LOVE WILL HAVE TO WAIT

Cressida Maitland expected her new job at the Carteret Foundation and going to live with her sister, Julia, to present challenges, but they were nothing compared with that of getting to know the devastatingly attractive Michael Carteret, business partner of Julia's fiancé, Tom. Cressida soon suspected that it was Julia in whom Mike was taking an interest. It wasn't until she finally understood the situation that the problems began in earnest. Would Mike ever trust her again?

MICHELLE GRAHAME

LOVE WILL HAVE TO WAIT

Complete and Unabridged

LINFORD
Leicester

First published in Great Britain in 1991 by
Robert Hale Limited
London

First Linford Edition
published 1998
by arrangement with
Robert Hale Limited
London

British Library CIP Data

Grahame, Michelle
   Love will have to wait.—Large print ed.—
Linford romance library
1. Love stories
2. Large type books
I. Title
823.9'14 [F]

ISBN 0–7089–5251–8

Published by
F. A. Thorpe (Publishing) Ltd.
Anstey, Leicestershire

Set by Words & Graphics Ltd.
Anstey, Leicestershire
Printed and bound in Great Britain by
T. J. International Ltd., Padstow, Cornwall

This book is printed on acid-free paper

To all those who had faith.

1

CRESSIDA MAITLAND surveyed her surroundings with a mixture of dismay and surprise. How could she have accumulated so much in such a comparatively short time.

She swept a conglomeration of half-used lipsticks, foundations and eye make-up into an already overflowing waste-bin and made a face in the dressing-table mirror. The discarded aids to beauty had mostly been cast-offs from Julia who spent much time trying to impress on her sister the benefits of cosmetics, but then she was an actress and always looking the part was her stock-in-trade. Cressida's face with its wide grey eyes, short nose and generous mouth, at least in its owner's opinion did not respond satisfactorily.

For perhaps the hundredth time she

wondered if the decision to live with her sister again was the right one but now that they were both older and because Julia had acquired a fiancé, she hoped that many of the reasons for their previous clashes had now been removed.

Two months ago Julia's letter had come out of the blue and it had been even more of a surprise when Cressida learned that her sister had bought a cottage with part of the proceeds of her latest film and actually wanted them to set up house together . . . 'and I've found the perfect job for you too!' the letter went on . . . 'it seems that the local orphanage wants a qualified child-care worker to start a new venture and of course I thought of you. I've enclosed all the details — I'm away quite a lot and it does seem a shame to leave the cottage empty.' Well, there was no going back now. She had applied for and got the job as nursery school superintendent at the Carteret Foundation, now all that remained was to create some sort of order out of the chaos, pack most of it into her ageing Mini and take leave of her landlady.

Because her family home was about halfway between the northern town that she had lived in for the past two years and the Sussex village where Julia's new cottage was situated, Cressida had decided to spend the night at the vicarage and then drive on the next day. There was no one in when she got there so she left a note on the hall table. 'Gone to see St Michael.'

The church, in contrast to the vicarage, was mediaeval and very beautiful, Cressida loved being able to slip into it alone, she particularly liked the great east window. It depicted the defeat of the dragon by St Michael and was a memorial to those who had fallen in two world wars. The artist had symbolized war and evil in the double headed monster now lying dead with the blade of a broken sword deep in its chest and St Michael, not as a saint but as a soldier, offering the hilt of the sword, as though it was a cross, to a group of angels bending down from heaven to receive it. For Cressida it was the face of the soldier that appealed to her, although the dragon had been defeated, his was not an air of triumph but of peace and acceptance as though the struggle had been almost more than he could endure. She loved his clear-cut features and the shine on his bronze-coloured hair. It was, in truth, to him that she had always come to share her troubles and her joys when everyone else seemed too busy. Later she had placed in him the ideals of manhood that she had hoped to find in a real person. A noise in the road broke into her thoughts and as she rose from the pew she whispered, "I know I'll find you one day."

The telephone was ringing when Cressida got back to the house. "Oh good, I'm so glad you're there." It was Julia. "Listen, Cress, I've phoned to tell you that we are going out to dinner tomorrow . . . I have to go up to town and there won't be time to get anything else organized. We're going to a super little restaurant called the Captain's Table in Seahaven, that's only a few miles on from Chanterhurst . . . I'll leave the key of the cottage under the mat so you can have a good look round and change and whatnot — and don't worry it isn't a formal 'do'. There'll only be Tom and his partner from the yard."

"Oh all right, Ju. What time then?" Cressida sighed resignedly.

"About 7.30 I think. I must fly now. Give my love to revered Papa. See you tomorrow." The phone went dead. Cressida replaced the receiver slowly. Typical Julia, she thought, she had been looking forward to settling in at the cottage, not dining with strangers, even if one of them was going to be Julia's fiancé, Tom Blakeney.

The front door opened and the Reverend Arthur Maitland came in. He rushed forward to hug his youngest daughter. "And how's my little chick? Looking well I see. I'm sorry I wasn't here when you arrived, pastoral duty called."

At tea, as Cressida was working her way through plates of home-made delights, the vicar broke the silence. "Are you looking forward to the change, Cressy?"

"Yes, Dad, I really think I am. I've had my doubts of course, and then when she phoned just now informing me that she had arranged a dinner-party for tomorrow, without so much as a 'by your leave' I thought, Oh no! What have I done!"

The vicar smiled. "You know, Cressy, you shouldn't be so quick to jump to conclusions, sometimes the wrong ones, you cause yourself a lot of trouble that way."

Cressida thought this over; finally she said, "I suppose Julia really thought that a proper dinner out was actually better than beans on toast at home."

"Exactly so, my dear. I believe that if

you try and understand her a bit more, you two will get along fine."

Cressida gave a little sigh. "I'm certainly going to give it my best shot. I really want it to work this time."

"That's my girl; now I must go and do some work. If you wouldn't mind doing the tea things?" Ten minutes later a head popped round the study door and Cressida announced she was going out for a walk.

At first she couldn't make up her mind which way to go and then almost without thinking she found herself on the farm track that wound round the bottom of Brandstone Hill. The motor-racing circuit that encircled the top of it was silent. She was about to ignore the half-hidden path that led up the hill, as she had done so many times before, but it seemed to draw her like a magnet. Wasn't now as good as time as any to face a past she had shunned and try to come to terms with it once and for all?

She began to climb the steep slope,

her feet frequently slipping on its wet surface. She could see through the half-bare trees, unlike that Summer afternoon nearly five years ago when the thick foliage hid her as she sat watching the cars scream past. She remembered how the heat had accentuated the unique atmosphere, an amalgam of hot rubber, burning exhaust and excitement. Then she had heard the distant drone of a quite different kind of engine, much deeper than a racing-car, nearer and nearer it came. Suddenly it turned to a screech of tyres, brakes and metal, then a moment of eerie silence, followed by the horrendous sound of trees being smashed as something huge crashed its way down the slope, and then silence again. Cressida recalled how she too had stood transfixed before coming to her senses and begin to scramble, run, and crawl towards the place where the noise had come from. There, lying three parts upside-down, was a huge eight cylinder, 3 litre Bentley, the rear wheels still turning, the front crumpled against one of the larger trees. The car had cut a great swathe through the woodland, smaller trees were snapped off, larger ones had branches hanging at crazy angles. The scene was one of total devastation.

Now, as she turned off the path and looked at the exact spot it was obvious that not even in five years had nature been able to repair all the damage done in those few dreadful seconds. There was still a large scar on the tree that the car had smashed into and that she had slithered round to find what she had been dreading, the driver trapped and bleeding underneath the vehicle, a red stain spreading rapidly across one leg.

Kneeling down beside him she had lifted the visor of his helmet, the fireproof mask maintaining anonymity; at least he was still breathing, but unconscious. A huge gash in his thigh was pumping out blood at a terrifying rate. Cressida prayed her first-aid course would pay off. She needed to apply pressure as quickly as possible. She found a hanky, not perfectly clean, but it would have to do, and then she thought of the small, flat package that Julia had asked her to collect from a local jeweller, she had no idea what was in it but it would provide the necessary pressure. She wrapped it in the hanky and pressed it firmly onto the wound, then kept it in place with the elastic snake-belt she had been wearing. Over this she wound the driver's own scarf.

She could do nothing for the other leg which was trapped up to the hip, and then she heard the welcome sound of sirens as a rescue team rushed to the scene, almost certainly alerted by another passing driver. Suddenly she had not wanted to become involved any further, no one noticed her as she slipped quietly away and back down the path . . .

Cressida had avoided the place ever since; now she wondered why. It had been a horrific reality at the time but it was in the past. It was time to leave it there. She reached the vicarage just as her father was emerging from his study. "Good walk?" he asked.

"I went up to the track at Brandstone again. I haven't been there since . . . oh well, you know . . . "

"What made you go today?"

"I'm not sure I can answer that, Dad, but I know now that even bad things seem better when they're faced."

Cressida had never told anybody, not even her father, the whole story of what had happened that afternoon. "Perhaps it's time you talked about it then."

"Later maybe . . . after dinner . . . ask me again then. I'm going up to change now. I'll have a bath — if the water's hot enough, that is."

As he watched her go up the stairs the vicar recalled the evening before Cressida's eighteenth birthday. The celebration dinner had turned into a disaster. Cressida had run into the house, going straight to the bathroom. This was followed by

Julia hammering on the door and screaming that Cressida was taking all the hot water. On the way to the restaurant there had been another scene between them when Julia discovered that Cressida had 'lost' the package she had been asked to collect. She had called her sister a careless cow, and was damned if she would ever buy her another present, because that is what the package apparently contained. Cressida had apologized but the two of them hardly spoke another word for the rest of the evening. Arthur had longed for the advice and comfort of his wife.

The next day Cressida had pleaded with him to use his position as chaplain to the local hospital to find out how a driver, injured at Brandstone the day before, was getting on. She had then, reluctantly, admitted that she had seen an accident at the track. "I'm sorry, my dear," he had had to report, "the driver brought in yesterday died an hour ago." The vicar brought his mind back to the present. Was he going to hear the whole story at last?

During dinner they talked mostly about Cressida's new job. "It's funded by a thing called the Carteret Foundation, which seems to be very well endowed. The idea is to integrate the children who live at the Foundation with children from the local community at pre-school age," she explained.

"Do you think it'll work?"

"I hope so but I got the distinct impression at the interview that not everyone there was in favour of the scheme . . . but it's sure to be very interesting."

It wasn't until they were having their coffee that Cressida unfolded the whole history of that Saturday afternoon five years ago. When she had finished he carefully replaced his cup on the table before speaking. "Why didn't you tell me all this before, Cressida? I could have helped you; or if not me then somebody better qualified. It never does any good to keep things like

13

this bottled up you know."

"Yes, I think I understand that now, but at the time I just couldn't face the awful fuss that there would have been. And then when I found out that he had died . . . it was all for nothing anyway. I had terrible feelings of guilt in case it was my fault."

"Oh, Cressida, my dear, these things are not for us to decide, we need the guidance of a higher authority, and we can get it you know . . . if we ask."

"I do know, Dad, my visits to St. Michael have always helped; perhaps it was seeing him today that finally decided me to talk about it . . . but only to you, I don't want anyone else to know . . . ever."

The vicar had one last question. "Did Julia ever tell you what your intended birthday present was?"

"No, she didn't, and I certainly wasn't going to ask!"

★ ★ ★

Due to a puncture which she had had to deal with herself it was nearly six o'clock before Cressida pulled up outside Lower End Cottage. At first glance it didn't seem very aptly named, since it stood high on a bank and was reached by two flights of steep narrow steps without handrails. She decided immediately only to take the barest necessities up to the cottage that night.

There wasn't time for much more than a wash and change before she had to set out again, for a dinner with strangers that she could well do without; but her first impression of the cottage was pleasing — plenty of hot water, combined with old-world charm.

She wished she had a better idea of what to wear. Julia's 'informal' could mean almost anything. In the end she chose a close-fitting black wool skirt and a black cowl-neck sweater. She lightened this by wearing cerise-coloured low-heeled pumps and tying her hair back with a velvet bow in the same shade, pinning a large gilt brooch onto her collar. Well, it would just have to do.

She picked up the card lying on her dressing-table. 'The Captain's Table', there was a little map printed on the back and words written in Julia's bold hand. 'See you there, love, J.' Nevertheless it was quite an effort to leave the cottage and climb back into the car.

2

THE drive to Seahaven took about twenty minutes but the restaurant was easy to find. Automatically, she looked round the car-park to see if there was any car that caught her eye. In one corner she spotted the Jaguar XJS, one of her favourites, its sleek shape and contained power always gave her a thrill. If she ever had that kind of money it would certainly be on her short list.

Cressida pushed open the door and for a moment the interior seemed dark compared to the well-lit car-park, the only brightness coming from a bar at the far end of the room. She looked round for any sign of Julia. Suddenly her gaze was arrested. There, seated at the bar, was her 'St. Michael of the east window'; one arm was raised, just as it was in the church, but now his hand held a glass, not a sword. The reflections of the red and green lights in the mirrors and glasses behind the bar resembled stained glass, and the silhouetted profile of the man made her knees want to do the strangest things.

The moment was shattered by a squeal of delight. "Cressy! Darling!" Julia's best dramatic tones not only penetrated her sister's consciousness but caused others to turn in their direction. Cressida hugged her sister and felt a delicate embrace in return, her senses overwhelmed by a waft of expensive perfume. "Wonderful to see you . . . and on time, too! I told Tom you wouldn't get lost; he thinks because you're my sister you must have my lousy sense of direction." She turned towards the bar. "Tom! Come and meet Cressy."

An enormous man unhitched himself from a barstool and came towards them; he put one huge hand on Julia's shoulder and held out the other. "The

18

little sister I've heard so much about . . . I'm delighted. Now come and meet Mike; our table will be ready in about fifteen minutes, just time for you to have a quick one."

Meeting Tom and Julia had put the vision of her east window out of her mind, so it was a second little shock when the three of them converged on the man whose face and attitude had so startled her in the first place.

She heard Julia say, "Cressy, this is Michael Carteret, Tom's partner at the boatyard." Cressida's hand was taken in a firm grip, but it was the man's eyes that held her attention. They seemed dark and penetrating but at the same time had a guarded quality she could not define. His smile of greeting was pleasant enough but only involved his well-shaped mouth, the eyes remained untouched. He made the conventional remarks about her journey and the weather, but while he was speaking Cressida was wondering about his name, surely Carteret was the name of the Foundation she was going to work for? She must find out before putting her foot in it. She enquired at once.

"Don't worry, Cressida, I'm not part of an advance vetting party," he laughed. "In fact I am one of the trustees of the Foundation but only because of my name. I have absolutely nothing to do with the running of the place, it was set up by my grandfather donkey's years ago. Now what would you like to drink?"

At this point Julia said. "Try a 'Captain's Special', Cress, they're terrific."

Tom signalled the barman. "Another 'Captain's Special' please, that is if you'd like to try one Cressida?"

"If Julia thinks they're terrific I expect I will too."

She turned as Mike said, "Do you always share the same tastes as Julia then?"

The question was asked casually but she felt that it was somehow a heavily loaded one. "Julia has very good taste don't you think?" Mike inclined his head as he handed her a glass filled with delicately-shaded liquid. She felt she had come out of that little encounter with equal honours and then immediately wondered why that seemed to be so important. A few minutes later a waiter arrived to tell them their table was ready.

"Listen you two," said Julia, "you go on to the table — Tom, you can take Cressida's drink — we'll make a quick visit to the 'ladies'. See you all in a minute." Despite Cressida's assurances that she was OK, Julia took her firmly by the arm and whisked her off. Although, as was customary wherever Julia went heads were turned, Cressida felt that there was one pair of eyes that were following her.

As soon as they were in the 'ladies', Julia asked eagerly. "Well, what do you think of Tom? Isn't he gorgeous? Is he what you expected? Well?" Julia leant forward in the mirror and pouted as she applied her lipstick, looking at her sister reflected there.

"From what I've seen, he seems very nice and certainly big enough — six feet four if he's an inch — and I suppose he's sort of reassuring, I should think you could depend on him in a crisis." Cressida replied carefully. Tom was quite different to the types that Julia usually had in tow, but none the worse for that. In her usual straightforward way she added, "he's a lot older than I expected, he must at least be ten years older than you."

Julia snapped her handbag shut and retorted almost as snappily. "Twelve, actually, if you must know. Is that all you've got to say?"

"Oh, for goodness sake, Ju, be reasonable! I've only just met the man, and apart from telling Dad that you'd found the man you wanted to marry, and that he owned a boatyard, you were pretty meagre with the information. I can see that you're in love with him and surely that's the most important thing?"

Julia calmed down. "I'm sorry, Cress, but I do so want you to like him too, he means so much to me . . . more than I ever believed any man could."

"I really am pleased for you. Now tell me about Mike . . . how well do you know him?" Cressida ran a comb through her hair and readjusted the bow.

Julia didn't reply for a few seconds. "I've seen him quite often, at the yard — he's very clever — he sees to the design and installation of the radar and things like that in the boats, but I don't really know him at all — not as a person, that is."

Before Cressida could stop herself she said. "Has he got a girlfriend or . . . or anything?".

Julia gave her sister a shrewd look. "If he had, don't you suppose she would be here now? Anyway what is it to you? You can hardly be interested in such a short space of time." Julia's voice held an edge to it. "Anyway I don't think you're his type." She gave herself a last glance in the mirror.

A waiter showed them to the table where Mike and Tom were already seated. Tom got up and helped Julia with her chair and the waiter did the same for Cressida.

The lighting in the restaurant was brighter than in the bar and Cressida could see that Mike did indeed have bronze-brown hair, darker underneath but almost touched with gold on the surface, like the highlights on a bronze sculpture and his eyes which had looked dark brown now seemed to be more of a greeny-brown shade. Sitting opposite him she could see that he had broad, powerful shoulders beneath the jacket of his well-cut suit.

"Do you like seafood, Cressida?" asked Tom, cutting in on her thoughts.

"Mmm, yes I do."

"Then I recommend the. 'Cabin Boy's Delight' which, despite its awful name, is a really good prawn and avocado cocktail with an unusual dressing." She decided to try it, followed by a chicken dish, the others chose steak and Tom ordered for everyone.

Cressida regaled them all with her tale of the flat tyre, managing to make it sound both awful and amusing at the same time. Throughout the telling she could not help but be aware of Mike's silent scrutiny.

During the course of the meal she discovered how Tom and Julia had met at the Boat Show when Julia was doing some personal appearance publicity for the film in which she and one of Tom's boats had starred.

"You've forgotten to tell her about the bit when I said, 'Who's that enormous creature who seems to think he owns the boat?' And one of the others there said, 'He *is* the enormous creature who owns the boat, shall I introduce you?' Everything just seemed to follow on from that . . . the cottage . . . the engagement, although that is still unofficial, only you and Dad and," she hesitated, "one or two others know about it."

"Were you at the Boat Show, Mike?"

"No, Cressida, I'm strictly a back-room boy — I leave the publicity angle to those . . . er . . . better equipped for the job." Cressida wasn't entirely sure what to make of that remark, to her he seemed ideally suited. The image of the 'east window' that had so startled her when she arrived was fast being replaced by a real man.

She liked his clear-cut features with their interesting planes and angles — she assessed him to be in his early thirties even although there were finely-etched lines round his mouth and dark-lashed eyes. But it was a face that didn't give much away, neither did he say a lot — leaving most of the conversation to the other three.

Over coffee he addressed Cressida directly. "What sort of things do you like to do in your spare time?"

Before she could answer Julia broke in . . . "Oh, Cressy's the outdoor type, walking, jogging, tennis, skiing, you name it, she does it . . . "

"Julia, no, you make it sound awful, as though I'm some sort of fitness fanatic."

"Anything less physical?" Cressida thought she detected a note of sarcasm in Mike's voice but she couldn't be certain. She narrowed her grey eyes and looked straight at him.

"I do a bit of sculpting but it takes time and space, commodities I've been a bit short of lately."

"She did that horse on the mantelpiece at the cottage, you remember it, Mike, don't you?" Julia remarked enthusiastically.

Mike gave Cressida a smile that reached all the way to his eyes as he replied, "Yes I do, I thought it was very good. You must like horses." The smile made Cressida suddenly feel that the world was a better place.

The party broke up shortly after that and Julia dragged her sister into the 'loo' once more where she began to repair her lipstick again. "Honestly, Ju, I hardly think you need to do that again at this late hour."

"Sorry, Cressy, just habit I suppose. I'm ready now."

Cressida was not surprised to find that the two men were already in the car-park — Tom was towering over the Mini. "How did you know which one was mine?" she asked.

"I didn't think there'd be many Minis with everything bar the kitchen sink stacked in them. If you like I'll just check the wheel-nuts for you. I'm not being chauvinist," he added hastily.

Cressida heard Mike calling to her across the tarmac; somehow it came as no surprise to find him sitting in the Jaguar she had admired earlier.

"Mmm . . . nice," she said, patting the top of it.

"You like cars then?"

"I admire good design and engineering, I wanted to go in for it but I got side-tracked."

Mike touched her hand as it rested on

28

the window-sill. "I think that's a pity." He turned her hand over in his and the sensation of his fingers on hers suddenly became almost unbearable; she wanted to snatch hers away and only just managed to control the impulse. "You have good hands for practical things."

"Yes, perhaps so. Oh, I think Tom has finished, I'd better go." This man was producing feelings in her that she didn't even want to think about. To his call of 'see you again soon', she just half turned and smiled. Tom and her sister said their 'goodnights' and exchanged quick kisses. Julia waved vigorously at the occupants of the Jaguar as they pulled out of the car-park.

Despite her long, tiring day, Cressida found sleep difficult. Images of Michael Carteret kept coming into her mind; he certainly hadn't gone out of his way to impress her and yet he had, she was thinking of those guarded greeny-brown eyes when she finally fell asleep.

★ ★ ★

Tom lived in a block of flats, part of a new development a little way outside Seahaven. After some minutes driving in silence Mike said, "That was a very special evening; I would like to try another. Do you suppose Julia will agree?"

"She might. Had you anything in mind?"

"I thought we might go sailing. What do you think?"

Tom turned the idea over. "Yes, I don't see why not, but there are limits, you know, Mike."

"I hardly need reminding of that, now do I?"

"I'll ask Julia and see what she says. But if the answer is 'no' then that will have to be the end of it."

"I can't expect more than that, Tom." As he spoke Mike pulled up outside the flats and let Tom out of the car. He sped off into the night, driving the powerful car with consummate skill through the narrow lanes.

Once Cressida had fallen asleep it was deep and dreamless. She was awakened by her sister's voice: "Come on sleepyhead, it's nearly ten o'clock."

"Oh, good heavens!" She opened her eyes and saw Julia standing by the bed bearing a cup, which she placed on the bedside table.

"You needn't expect this treatment every morning, Cressy, but I felt a little guilty about last night, making you go out when you'd only just arrived."

"Well don't, I enjoyed it . . . really," she added as she saw Julia's raised eyebrow, "and I think your Tom is very nice." Cressida stretched her arms then leant over to take the tea.

Julia went over to the window and pulled back the curtains, then came and sat on the bed. "What have you got planned for today?"

"I've got to get all my things unpacked first, that should occupy what's left of the morning, and then

31

I thought I might explore the village — something like that — unless you've got a better idea."

Julia seemed relieved. "No; actually, darling, Tom and I are going up to town; he's got a client and I'm seeing my agent. He thinks he may have some TV for me. I don't know what exactly, but he hinted at a classic serial. Oh, Cressy, if it is, wouldn't that be marvellous!"

"I bet you'll get it, Julia; I know you're good, even in 'Spies Ahoy'. Talking of which, why wasn't Tom at the première, it was his boat after all?"

"He was invited but he was in the States at the time and Mike wouldn't go to anything like that anyway."

It was just the opening Cressida wanted. "Do you ever see Mike socially?" She tried to sound casual but judging by the look Julia gave her, hadn't succeeded.

"No, not much; the three of us have been out for dinner once before . . . no, twice," she corrected herself, "counting the time he came here for a meal. That was when he admired your sculpture. He has his own house but I don't think he entertains much." Julia paused. "I hope you're not going to get interested in that direction."

"Oh, Ju, I don't know — there's something about him that I found very attractive, but I got the distinct impression that I had no such effect on him, quite the reverse in fact. Don't tell Tom about this . . . promise?"

"Don't be stupid, Cress," Julia replied shortly.

It was time to drop the subject. She got up and went over to the window to look at the garden in proper daylight for the first time. It sloped gently up from the cottage. There was a small terrace with a pergola. This area was fairly tidy but as the land receded it became more overgrown. There was one large apple-tree and at the far end Cressida could see an ivy-covered stone wall. It was a challenge that just cried out to be met.

"Oh, Ju, I know what I'd like to do — make a start on the garden — you don't mind do you?"

"Silly," her sister replied affectionately. "You know that's one of the reasons I asked you here in the first place," she teased.

"There's one thing that puzzles me, Julia. Why don't you live here with Tom?"

"There are reasons, very good ones," Julia answered her sister seriously, "and I will tell you soon, I promise, but now I must fly. Tom will be here in an hour to pick me up and I haven't even changed."

"No, you certainly haven't, if it takes you that long!"

"Pig!" retorted Julia as she left the room.

★ ★ ★

Cressida was just carrying the last of her belongings through the hall when the telephone started to ring. Balancing the pile of books between one hand and her chin she managed to lift the receiver. "Hello!"

"This is Mike Carteret: is that Cressida?" She assented. "Look, I'm in a bit of a hurry, but if I asked you out to dinner, Cressida, would you come?"

Oh boy, would I, she thought! Now keep calm, don't make an idiot of yourself. To give herself more time she said, "Could you hold on a minute, Mike? I've got an armful of books and they're just about to cascade onto the floor . . . That's better, now please ask me again."

"Come to dinner with me next Saturday."

"Yes, I'd like that."

"Good, I'll pick you up at the cottage — about sevenish. Oh, and it definitely won't be a dressy affair . . . I mean that!" He made the remark seem slightly mysterious but he rang off before she could comment.

Cressida admitted to herself that the

invitation was just what she had been hoping for, and yet it had been issued in the briefest, most casual of tones. Had she sounded too keen, accepted too quickly? Hell's bells! How could being in the company of a man for only two hours be so disturbing? An afternoon's hard work in the garden did much to restore her perspective even if it seemed to have little effect on the weeds.

★ ★ ★

Mike, the cottage garden and any other thoughts couldn't have been further from her mind next day as she drove to 'Sandilands', the house where the Carteret Foundation had its headquarters. Cressida knew that the job she had been employed to do was neither the brainchild nor the desire of Mrs Sinclair, the administrator, and she was under no illusion that fulfilling the aims of the trustees would be easy.

Mrs Sinclair's greeting was polite but

cool. "I feel it only fair to you, Miss Maitland, to make it clear that I am against this experiment in community relations."

"Don't you think a scheme that gives the children a chance of finding permanent homes to be of value?"

"If it would, I might, but I don't believe it will," was the cold reply. A girl came in carrying a tray. "I have asked Sarah to join us for coffee as she will be working with you in the nursery school." Oh Lord, thought Cressida, already she has an ally and a spy in my camp.

The nursery school unit was in a separate modern building; Cressida was delighted with the amenities. There were two well-furnished classrooms with almost everything in them that she could possibly want, money could do so much. The school had been running for a number of years, but until now had only been available for children who lived in the Foundation homes; it would be Cressida's job not only to initiate the integration with outside families but she would have an important PR role to accomplish as well. Sarah showed her the office. "Have you got a list of all the new enrolments?"

The girl pointed to a filing cabinet in the corner. "I think you'll find everything you need in there . . . the keys are in the desk drawer."

"Good, then I'll see you at 8.45 tomorrow." She gave Sarah an encouraging smile.

If Cressida was disappointed by her reception at the Foundation, she certainly couldn't fault their paperwork, all the information she wanted, even down to the first fortnight's menus, was contained in the files.

★ ★ ★

Julia had received the news of Mike's invitation with a noticeable lack of enthusiasm. "I can't understand you, Ju," said Cressida exasperatedly. "You

38

were always so keen in the past for me to find someone of my own to go out with. What's wrong now? He's not a sex maniac or anything, is he?" She was joking, but the feeling that Julia was being less than open with her niggled away at the back of her mind.

"Oh, it's just that you haven't had time to make any friends down here yet. I don't think you should get involved before you've had time to look the field over, so to speak. Tom knows heaps of other people; if you came out with us you'd meet some of them."

"I'd hardly call going out to dinner with someone getting involved, Julia. Anyway I'm going, so there! And he's calling for me at seven." She looked at her watch. "Heavens! I'd better get a move on!"

Quarter of an hour passed and most of Cressida's wardrobe was scattered across the room. Finally she chose a jacket and trousers in navy cord with matching accessories and a crimson silk shirt — by the time she had powdered her nose and added a touch of lipstick a shade lighter than the blouse, leaving her hair loose, she could hear the front door opening. She dashed down the stairs expecting to find Mike in the hall, but it was Julia who had gone down the steps and was standing at the open passenger door, not of the Jaguar that Cressida had been hoping for, but of a smart, motorized caravan.

"I heard Mike arrive, darling, so I thought I'd just come out and tell him you were nearly ready." Was that what it was, thought Cressida, unable still to rid herself of the suspicion that there was something going on that she didn't understand. But Julia quickly moved away to allow Cressida to climb up into the vehicle, then retreated up the steps, waving them off. "Have a good time, you two."

As she clicked home the seat-belt she found herself saying rather weakly, "I'm sorry if I kept you waiting." She threw a surreptitious glance at Mike to try and make out what he was wearing; he intercepted it and grinned.

"Yes . . . you're OK . . . and very nice too," he added.

"How did you . . . ?"

"It's always the first thing any woman wants to know. 'Am I wearing the right clothes?' Mike was in dark slacks, a beige cashmere polo-neck and a brown suede jacket — he was just as attractive as she remembered. Her senses were assailed by the faintest hint of a spicy aftershave. It reminded her that she had meant to apply some of the expensive perfume that Julia had given her for Christmas but typically had forgotten.

"I expect you are wondering about the Jag?"

"Well I must admit I was looking forward to it."

"I need a van for what we're going to do this evening!"

For a moment Cressida's worst fears and Julia's veiled warnings flashed through her mind. Then she saw the amusement in Mike's dark eyes as laugh-lines creased the corners of them, and was instantly reassured. She sat back to enjoy the drive through unfamiliar countryside and the company of the most intriguing man she had ever met.

3

IT was a beautiful April evening and the route was through winding Sussex lanes, their hedges newly greened. In the woodlands, birch, oak and beech were just beginning to show their summer finery and beneath them the sapphire carpet of bluebells lay unrolled.

"I do love this time of year." Cressida wound the window down so that she could feel the sweetness of the air. "Nature does the same thing every year but for some reason it's just as exciting each time."

"Except that every time you're a year older!"

"Oh Mike! That's a terrible thing to say. Something good should be enjoyed for what it is."

"You're an idealist, I'm a realist."

"That's no excuse for not taking

43

pleasure in the good things of life, just because they may not last."

Mike changed his tack. "You at least can't conceal your enthusiasm for them, Cressida."

She thought for a few moments. "I don't believe it's a question of 'can't', Mike. Feelings should be expressed, sometimes sad ones as well as happy ones."

"And do you think that feelings about people should be expressed so spontaneously?"

"Ah," she said, a little frown creasing her forehead, "that can be quite a different matter; it can take much longer to find out about people; hasty judgements can sometimes be disastrous."

"So you don't believe in 'love at first sight', for instance?"

Cressida gave him a quick glance but could make nothing of his bland expression. "Now I think you're teasing me." She certainly didn't want to get involved in that sort of conversation.

Mike suddenly changed the subject again. "I don't think Julia is much of a country lover, is she? I can't see her spoiling her image with wellies and raincoats."

"Actresses are always conscious of their image, it's part of their training, and she's not as self-centred as you're trying to make out." Cressida paused and then added. "And of course she's very beautiful."

"Does that make a difference then?"

"Well yes . . . yes it does. You see people pay homage to her kind of perfection — they want to serve it — to preserve it, perhaps. She mustn't get her feet wet or her hands dirty or her hair windblown or be kept waiting; all her life she has accepted these things as her right, she takes them for granted. It's not a conscious selfishness, it's just the way the world treats beautiful things."

Mike slowed down and turned the van into an even narrower lane hardly more than a track in fact and without a proper surface. It wound steeply upwards. He didn't speak for a little, then said. " . . . and is Tom to be just another worshipper at this temple of beauty?"

Immediately Cressida's temper blazed. "Oh, I see what it is now. I've not been asked out by Michael Carteret but by the 'Tom Blakeney Protection Society!'" Anger and disappointment flowed through her in equal amounts. The vehicle came to a halt but she kept her head down, hiding her face with a curtain of blonde hair. She had hoped so much that this man's interest had been for herself alone.

Instead of the sarcastic remark or angry retort she had expected, Cressida heard him say in a quiet, almost tender tone, "I'm sorry, I apologize . . . both for seeming to pry about your sister and for giving the impression that I'd asked you out with an ulterior motive . . . forgive me?"

She glanced up and saw that his words were accompanied by an unexpectedly anxious expression . . . "If you forget what I just said in return . . . please." She was rewarded by seeing the worry fade and being replaced by a smile.

"It's a deal. Now will you give your attention to the place where I have brought you to dine." Cressida looked out through the windscreen. Mike had brought the van to rest a few yards from the edge of a hill which overlooked a little valley. One side was lit by the last rays of the setting sun, she could see sheep dotted about in hedge-contained fields, and smaller white dots indicate the presence of lambs. There were little green copses and fingers of oakwood spreading down the valley sides. A line of willows and the occasional silver flash of water showed that the place had its own little stream which widened out to form a small lake. The only buildings were set back from the lake and were built of mellow pink brick, bathed in evening light. She was speechless. "Well?" Mike questioned at last.

"Oh, Mike, it's just perfect!" She exclaimed, finally able to express herself. "Where is it? Whose is it?"

"It's just a place I know . . . and am very fond of. I often come up here just to look, and although technically this is a public byway very few people ever use it, so I can usually enjoy it in solitude."

"If you like to be alone here why did you bring me?"

He didn't answer her question at once, and when he did the deep tone she had heard in his voice before returned. "Because I was sure you were the sort of person who would like it too . . . and I was right, wasn't I?"

Impulsively she put her hand over his as it lay on the steering-wheel. "Thank you, Mike," she said quietly, then she felt his knuckles tighten under her touch and sensed an immediate withdrawal. Her hand dropped.

The mood was gone with his next words. "Now I have things to do, and while I am doing them I want you to do something for me." As he spoke he was searching around in the glove compartment and finally produced several lumps of sugar. "These are for a friend of mine, you will find him in a field at the end of that path." He pointed to a small opening between the trees. "It's about 150 yards but there's plenty of light left, you won't get lost."

Cressida was puzzled. "You mean you want me to go along there, alone, then give these to your . . . er . . . friend?"

"Yes, that's right," he nodded. "And when you come back I want to know how he looks and whether he's wearing his clothes, it still gets chilly at night. By the way his name is Horace and he is very gentle." Mike leant across and opened the passenger door to let Cressida out.

Just before reaching the trees she turned back to wave but Mike was no longer in the driver's seat. The path was dry and springy for the most part.

It sloped gently downwards, eventually ending at a stile and gate. At first the little field appeared to be empty, then in the far corner she saw a large chestnut horse quietly cropping the first growth of spring grass. "Horace!" she called tentatively. The horse looked up then started to trot towards her making little snorting noises. He pulled up at the stile, ears forward expectantly. Cressida offered him a lump of sugar, holding it on the flat of her hand. The horse nuzzled it up gently between his lips. He had two white socks in front and a white star on his forehead, he was wearing a green canvas rug and was unshod. Giving him the last of the sugar and a final pat she started back up the path.

In the quickening dusk, lights now shone out from inside the motorvan, as she approached, the rear doors opened and she could see Mike sitting at the end of one of the red bench seats. "Dinner is served, my lady!" He held out his arm to help her up the high step into the van and she could feel the strength of powerful muscles as she climbed in.

The back of the caravan had been transformed. A table was laid with snow-white napery and the soft gleam of silver in candle-light. "This is absolutely fantastic, Mike," she exclaimed. "You seem determined to amaze me!" He appeared highly delighted with her response. Even more so when she discovered a menu card in a silver holder: salmon mousse, boeuf en croûte, compôte of fruit, coffee and 'vin du van' with an exclamation mark after it! Each dish had been beautifully illustrated in miniature and beside her plate was a single red rosebud.

There was no proper kitchen in the van but between the driving-area and the back were built in a small cooker, fridge and sink, all within arm's reach of the diners. Mike took two plates of mousse from the fridge and another of melba toast and placed them on the table. Cressida tucked the crimson rose into her buttonhole; it matched her silk shirt exactly. "That was just good luck," Mike laughed as he noticed the coincidence. "Now tell me about my friend Horace. Did he look OK?"

"He seemed fine. I'm not an expert though. Is he yours?"

Mike hesitated slightly. "No, just an old friend."

Cressida thought she detected a note of sadness. "You wanted to know if he was wearing his 'clothes'." Mike nodded. "He had on a rug, I think it's called a 'New Zealand', but he wasn't shod."

"Do you ride?" he asked.

"As little girls Julia and I had a Shetland pony, but a vicar's stipend doesn't really run to extras like riding-lessons. Anyway there wasn't much time after Mother died."

"Do you miss her a lot?"

"Of course I did at first, and still do at times but I think Julia found it harder to come to terms with. You may find that difficult to believe, she presents such an invulnerable image to the world."

"We all have things we want to hide sometimes, don't you think?" Cressida was about to disagree when she remembered all the years she had kept the incident at Brandstone to herself, so she said nothing. Mike replaced their empty plates with two more from the oven.

"The mousse was delicious — may I ask who the chef is?"

"Not guilty, I'm afraid, I have a good lady who cooks and cleans. But I have to admit to the table arrangements. The van, incidentally, belongs to the firm. We use it at regattas and exhibitions."

During the meal their conversation covered many topics although Cressida felt that Mike was drawing her out and giving very little information about himself in return. At least she was having the opportunity to study his features more closely — she found him every bit as attractive as before. She had a sudden desire to run her fingers through his bronze hair, and the idea brought a flush to her cheek which she hoped he hadn't noticed. The candlelight softened the lines etched round the corners of his mouth but revealed deep shadows under his eyes, as though he didn't get enough sleep.

"How about some music?" he suggested as they finished their coffee. "You'll find a selection of tapes under the dashboard."

Cressida squeezed between the seats. "OK. What would you like?" She held out a handful of cassettes.

"Ah, no, the whole point of this is for you to choose." He looked at her sternly. "You see this is how I decide whether or not to ask a girl out again, it all depends on her choice of music!" He was joking of course, she could see the amusement in his eyes, and yet it was just something else that he used to keep her off balance. She took her time looking through all the tapes. She smiled to herself as she slipped her choice into the player and the strains of the Moonlight Sonata began to permeate the van.

"Come and sit here beside me?" She hesitated. "It's all right, I won't bite . . . or anything else!" She edged round the table and slid into the bench beside him. He tucked a tartan travelling rug round her knees. "There now, you won't get cold while I explain my points system." He grinned at her puzzled look. "It goes like this; people who choose Beethoven get 11 points — 10 for good taste, 1 for daring; Mozart gets 12; and so on . . . "

"So I haven't made an earth shattering choice then have I? Dull old Cressida!" Her voice and expression were ones of total innocence. Mike was just about to say something when the music paused for a second, then the strains of Mozart's Horn Concerto filled the vehicle.

For a moment he looked really surprised, then burst out into full-throated laughter. "You must have found one of Tom's tapes, 'Ten Great

Classics' or something. I think you've beaten the system!" Cressida joined in the laughter.

The drive back to the cottage seemed to take no time at all and as soon as he pulled up he leant across to open her door; as he drew back she had the feeling that he deliberately let his lips brush across her hair just above the temple, but the action was so swift and delicate she certainly couldn't swear to it. Cressida would have liked to prolong the moment, but the door was open and there was nothing else she could do but get out.

"Thank you, Mike for a perfect evening and a most unusual one." She put every ounce of genuine sincerity into her voice, longing for him to ask her for another date, but he seemed to have withdrawn into himself again.

"I'm glad you enjoyed it," was all he said as he started the engine and put it into gear. She was forced to close the door. Damn the man, why can't he be . . . be . . . ? suddenly she didn't know herself what she wanted him to be. She stood watching the tail-lights disappear into the night. He could have seen me to the door though," she thought, piqued by his apparent indifference.

★ ★ ★

Cressida had expected to lie in bed going over every aspect of the evening in her mind but instead she must have fallen asleep the moment her head hit the pillow because the next thing she was aware of was the shrill ringing of a bell. She turned over to put the alarm off, only to find that it wasn't on — the sound was coming from downstairs — of course, it was Sunday, and the telephone was ringing. She had just opened the bedroom door to go and answer it when she heard Julia's voice.

"Hello . . . just a moment, I'll get her . . . Oh, I see . . . Mmm, I don't know, Mike . . . but Mike darling this charade just can't go on, it's not fair

on any of us, particularly Cressida
. . . What does Tom say . . . Oh, I
see . . . Well this is the last time as far
as I'm concerned, it's bound to end in
disaster for someone."

The stab of jealousy that Cressida
felt curled her insides into a tight,
painful ball. For a moment she didn't
even hear Julia's shout of "It's for
you, Cressy," and when it came again
she could hardly respond. Instead she
grabbed her robe and ran downstairs.
The receiver was lying unattended on
the hall table and for a moment she was
tempted to replace it without speaking
but her native common sense prevailed;
after all half of any conversation can be
misinterpreted. "Yes?" she said, a little
guardedly.

Mike apologized for getting her out
of bed. "I somehow didn't expect you
to be a late riser."

"I'm not, as a rule, it's all that good
food and wine I had last night."

"How about trying something a bit
more energetic? Come sailing with me.

Have you ever sailed before?"

"No, never."

"Good, I fully expected to hear that you were Olympic standard! Does the idea appeal?" The urge to be with him overcame the fears that she was being used by a man whose real interest was in Julia. "Well?" Mike's voice broke into her thoughts and she realized she hadn't answered.

"I don't know, Mike, I might be seasick or something."

"We shan't find out till we try. How about Wednesday, about 5.30; if the weather's OK, that is? Julia will tell you where to go. I'm not going to take 'no' for an answer." Cressida gave in. "Great!"

As soon as he had gone, the dreadful sense of foreboding flooded back. It was no good, she just had to find out about the conversation between Mike and her sister. "Julia!" she called.

"In here, in the kitchen!" She went through to the tiny but modernized cottage kitchen, to find Julia making coffee and eating a piece of toast and honey. She put the two mugs on a tray with another plate of toast. "Come into the sitting-room, Cressy, I'm dying to hear all about your dinner with Mike. Where did you go? What did you have to eat?" She chattered on so normally that Cressida began to wonder if she had imagined the phone conversation, but it gave her the chance she wanted.

"Didn't he tell you, then? You talked for long enough before you called me. What was it all about?"

Without a second's hesitation and through a mouthful of toast Julia replied. "The yom-lub-ba . . . Sorry!" She swallowed, then enunciated in her best drama academy manner, "The Yacht Club Ball."

Cressida was taken by surprise. "What about it?"

"Mike can't make up his mind whether to go or not. First he said he wouldn't, now he's said he might, but not definitely. It's a real nuisance."

60

"Why?" The whole affair was becoming more and more incomprehensible to her sister.

"You see Tom is a vice-commodore of the club and he has a table to fill. If Mike doesn't come you will have no partner, so Tom will have to find someone else. If he doesn't do so soon he won't be able to get anyone, and by that I mean a presentable unattached male."

A great weight seemed to be lifted from the area of Cressida's chest. She knew her sister well enough to know why she would describe a minor social problem like that as a 'disaster'. It wasn't only the hot coffee that gave her a warm glow inside.

★ ★ ★

The first full week at the school did not begin very auspiciously. In various subtle ways Cressida's plans were frustrated and she was eventually obliged to call Sarah Whittle into the office and point out to her, in what she hoped sounded like firm but reasonable tones that her wishes were to be carried out.

It was also time to start meeting the parents of the children from outside the Foundation. She saw little Emma Jones walking round the play area hand in hand with one of the resident children. Mrs Jones would be as good as any to start with. She turned out to be very co-operative. Cressida hoped that all the mums would be as helpful.

"There is one more thing I'd like to know, Mrs Jones. How did you come to hear of the Foundation and especially of this school?"

"Everyone in these parts knows about the Foundation, Miss Maitland. As to the school — that was through my husband really. Well he works in Seahaven at a boatyard called Blakeney's." Cressida was very interested now. But surely Mike had said that he never had anything to do with the Foundation. Mrs Jones went on: " . . . Mr Tom Blakeney, that's my husband's boss, knew that I'd been offered a little job in the mornings but I couldn't take it unless I could find the right place for Emma. So Mr Tom suggested this new nursery as was starting soon."

Cressida was astonished, this was not what she had expected. "Mr Tom Blakeney?" she queried.

"Yes and of course that was good enough a recommendation for us."

"Being your husband's employer."

"Well that too — but mostly 'cos of his own son being a weekly boarder here."

There are times when even professional training is not enough to disguise pure shock. To hide what she felt must be showing in her face, Cressida bent down and opened a filing drawer, thoughts rushing through her mind like an express train. Tom had a son . . . had he also had a wife . . . got a wife even . . . Was he divorced? . . . widowed? . . . What did Julia think?

Oh God! Did Julia *know*? She shut the drawer with a bang, took a deep breath and returned to the conversation. She pretended that her search through the files had been to look for the name Blakeney. "There isn't anybody in the school of that name, Mrs Jones."

"Oh no, Miss Maitland, he would be old enough for primary school by now." Cressida longed to ask more questions but could find no justification for doing so. She would have to find out from Julia. She prayed silently that it wasn't going to be the most awful mess. Mrs Jones left, quite unaware of the turmoil she had created.

Cressida's prayers certainly weren't answered when she returned to the cottage that evening. There was one of Julia's notes by the phone. 'Gone up to town for a part!!! Staying with Suzannah to do some shopping. Back Thursday.' She took her frustration out on some unfortunate scrambled eggs and had just slapped them onto the toast when the phone rang.

"Hello . . . Oh Mike! Thank goodness!" Cressida couldn't keep the relief out of her voice.

"Listen, Cressida, I'm afraid we're going to have to postpone Wednesday's sailing expedition. I'm awfully sorry but I just can't make it."

She made a little intake of breath. "Oh well, never mind . . . another time perhaps."

"Surely, but at the moment I can't say when. I'll let you know as soon as possible." Typically, he offered no reason for the change of plan but he sounded genuine enough.

"There is something you could help me with, Mike, if you've got a moment to spare?"

He seemed a little cagey as he replied, "I will if I can . . . shoot."

"I wouldn't ask you, but Julia's away and I'm very worried. At the Foundation today I discovered that Tom has a son, so naturally I'm concer . . ."

" . . . Of course, you would be,"

Mike cut in. "Julia should never have left you to find out like that. I can put your mind at rest on one score anyway: Tom is a widower and perfectly free to marry, and Julia's fully aware of all the circumstances."

She gave a tremendous sigh of relief. "Thank you for telling me Mike, these last few hours have been hell . . . and then to find Julia away when I got back; you can imagine how I felt."

"You'll have to get the rest of the story from her, it's not really my business." Mike's tone suggested that he had said all he was prepared to say on the subject . . . again that reserve was apparent . . . "I'll let you know as soon as the sailing can be organized. Goodbye, take care."

Her only thought when Julia returned, laden with boxes and bags bearing expensive names, was to start questioning her at once about Tom and his son.

"Why didn't you tell me Tom had been married before, Julia? . . . and had a son? I was flabbergasted. You could have said something, you know," she added somewhat resentfully.

"Yes, I suppose I should, I didn't think; I was going to of course. Who told you anyway?"

"A Mrs Jones, whose husband works at Blakeney's and whose child goes to the nursery."

"Oh Lord! I didn't think of it getting about like that. Everyone seems to know everyone else's business here.

"You of all people, Julia, should know that, coming from a village like Dunster . . . and being a vicar's daughter!"

"Well I'm sorry, Cress. I'll make up for it now by telling you the whole story."

"Good." Cressida was still not wholly appeased. "I was worried to death until Mike told me that Tom was a free man, so to speak . . ."

Julia gave a hoot of laughter. "Dear little sister, did you think I'd got myself all tied up with a married man? You should know me better than that. Did

Mike tell you anything else?"

"Not a thing, he said it was your business, not his."

"Typical. Well, be that as it may, here goes. You might get us both a drink first." Cressida poured out two sherries as quickly as she could.

"Tom told me he was a widower almost as soon as we met, and a little while later he told me about Andrew, who is just five, by the way. A few days later he told me about Lucy . . . "

"Lucy!" Cressida could hardly believe her ears.

"Yes, Lucy. She's eight now, and lives with his late wife's people in Hampshire." Cressida said nothing. "It took much longer to find out what happened to his wife, how she died I mean. She was nearly eight months pregnant when she had a fall, and although she appeared to be otherwise unhurt, it started the baby coming. She was rushed to hospital, Andrew was born, a bit early but perfectly OK. Then without warning, Anna became unconscious and died a few days later."

"Oh God, how awful — poor Tom."
Cressida thought how wrong one can
be about other people's lives, even
one's own sister's. The Julia of old
would never have contemplated taking
on a ready-made family.

"Let's have a refill," Julia suggested
and took Cressida's glass. "Now you
understand why Tom and I couldn't
live here, it wouldn't be right for the
children; but before you say anything
else, yes, we do sleep together, but only
at Tom's flat and never if Andrew's
there."

"Well I think you're very brave
tackling such a problem. Here's to you,
Julia," said Cressida, raising her glass.

"We all have problems to face
sometimes, so here's to you overcoming
yours," her sister replied.

"What problems?"

"Oh, who knows?" At that moment
the telephone rang and Julia got up
to answer it. A little later she popped
her head round the door and said,

"It's Tom, he's got a message for you from Mike. Can you manage tomorrow, same time, same place?" Cressida nodded vigorously and felt that at that moment she didn't have a care in the world.

Julia did not reappear for some twenty minutes and then with the news that the four of them would go on to a local pub called 'The Smugglers' when the sail was over.

All next day Cressida was on tenterhooks, she kept looking out of the window to see what the weather was doing. It had been quite windy in the morning — by the evening it seemed to her to be perfect — sun and a light breeze.

Because there was no time for her to go back to the cottage to change, she had brought with her what she hoped was suitable gear for the occasion, heavy cotton slacks in a bright turquoise blue and a thick Aran-knit polo-neck sweater, she put on socks and trainers and made a single plait of her hair.

By following Julia's directions she had no difficulty in finding the marina. Mike's Jag was already there and halfway down the jetty she saw the figure of Tom Blakeney. In one hand he held an orange life-jacket while the other was occupied steadying a small boat with a boat-hook. Mike was sitting in the stern, he looked up and waved.

Cressida had a sudden attack of cold feet, a condition she was thoroughly unaccustomed to. Normally she accepted gladly the challenge of a new experience. Now she felt afraid of making a fool of herself in front of a man whose good opinion of her had become so important. To chicken out now, however, would be even worse.

"Hi there, Cressida!" Tom held out the life-jacket. "I'm afraid you've got to wear this, it's one of the club rules." She saw that Mike was also wearing one over a navy sweater and jeans tucked into seaman's boots. Tom talked about the perfect weather as she put it on, then he checked the straps.

Mike called from the boat, "You look fine, Cressida. Just one thing though, I'd take the socks off. Little boats like this always have some water slopping about in the bottom, if your feet get wet they act like a wick and soak your legs."

Give them to me and I'll let Julia have them, Tom volunteered. She handed over the offending garments wondering why she felt like one of her own nursery school children caught in some unacceptable act. Godammit, she thought, he only told me . . . no . . . suggested, that I take my socks off!

Tom handed her into the boat and Mike indicated where she should sit. For the next five minutes he explained carefully and clearly what the various parts of the boat were called. He told her what to do in the unlikely event of a capsize and was glad to discover that she was a good swimmer. "Nevertheless," he emphasized strongly, "you must not leave the boat. Rescue-parties can find an upturned boat much more easily than a lone swimmer. Now it's time we got under way. Cast off forrard Tom."

Tom unhitched the rope and pushed the bow out with the boat-hook. Mike moved the tiller, the sails fluttered and filled then suddenly the jetty was left behind.

"Have a good sail!" Tom's voice followed them.

Cressida quickly learned the various moves to make when Mike made the boat change tack. At first she was too uptight really to enjoy the sensation but at least she didn't feel at all sick, as she had feared. Mike, on the other hand, seemed very relaxed and she sensed in him a freedom of spirit that had somehow been lacking before. Gradually she became less tense and under his gentle but firm tuition was persuaded to take control of one of the sails. He let her take the tiller after they had rounded a buoy and were running with the wind. She was surprised how lively it was, and from time to time he put his hand over hers to steady it. "Tell me, Cressida, are you enjoying it?"

She looked at him seriously, feeling that her reply mattered to him. "Yes, but I'd like to know more about it before I commit myself, Mike."

"That's an honest answer at least. In that case I'll try and get someone from the club to give you some lessons." His words were shattering. Once again he seemed to get closer, only to veer off at the last minute. Why didn't he want to be the one to give her the lessons? Cressida tried hard not to let his rejection of her as a pupil spoil the rest of the outing, concentrating so hard on the management of her sail that she was surprised to see that the jetty was quite close, with Tom and Julia waiting for them there.

When they were within earshot, her sister called out. "You didn't manage to capsize it then, Cress!"

"She did very well, Julia; better

than most first-timers, I'd say." Mike replied, running the mainsail down. He threw the mooring-rope to Tom who was ready with the boat-hook.

"She always does well at things needing physical co-ordination." Cressida couldn't help wondering why her sister was always so keen to impress upon everyone that she was some kind of sporting superwoman.

Mike suggested. "You know, Tom, I think we might ask Bob Burton to take her out. He'll be looking for a crew this year, now that Liz is expecting."

"Come on, Cressy, let's leave the men to discuss your scintillating future and put their boat to bed. We'll go on to 'The Smugglers' and you can be changed by the time they get there." Once in the car Julia asked. "How did you really get on with the sailing, and Mike?"

"The sailing was OK but Mike doesn't even want to take me out again. Oh Julia, I don't know what to think, one minute he's so nice and the next he pushes me away . . . Can't you give me *any* idea what makes him tick?" Cressida asked despairingly.

"Look, sis, I've told you before and I'll say it again. I hardly know the man. The longest talk I've ever had with him was when he came to dinner at the cottage and somehow he managed to find out all about me and give very little in exchange."

Cressida nodded; she recognized the experience. "Why haven't you asked him to the cottage more often, with Tom of course?"

"Oh well, he finds it very difficult to . . . " Julia stopped abruptly, then seemed to cover up quickly . . . "to get much time for socializing, he's away on business so much." Cressida frowned; she was sure her sister had been going to reveal something important and had only just stopped herself in time, but it wouldn't be any good pursuing it — she wasn't an actress for nothing.

4

BY the time they got there the pub car-park was full and they had to drive to the nearest public one. Walking back, Cressida thought she saw Mike's Jag pulling up in the narrow High Street but Julia practically pushed her through the door and bustled her into the 'ladies' to change. She had brought a cream silk shirt and a caramel-coloured blouson suit in fine wool, with a wide, black patent-leather belt and high heeled shoes to match. She undid the plait and pinned her hair up in a French knot, allowing a few tendrils to curl onto her neck.

When they emerged Cressida could see that the main lounge was divided into two levels, the upper had a long bar and a huge inglenook fireplace, the lower was divided into booths by dark panelling. Tom was waiting for them at the foot of the three steps that led from the upper to the lower lounge.

"I've ordered for you, Julia, but what would you like Cressida?" Mike was taking the drinks handed down from the upper lounge by the barman.

"I'd like a half of lager please, Tom. Mike passed the order on as she slid into the booth opposite him. "You were right, this is a lovely pub, is it your local?"

Tom and Mike both spoke together. "Yes . . . No," they contradicted. Everyone laughed.

"You'll have to explain that," Cressida insisted.

Mike took it up. "You see it lies about midway between where we all live — so it's easy to meet here . . . Have you studied a map of the area yet?" She shook her head. "I've got one at the office if you'd like to borrow it."

"Oh, I think I ought to buy one of my own." The reply was intended to be purely practical but as soon as she had uttered it she could see that she had snubbed him.

From his tone as he said, "Yes perhaps that would be better," she knew he felt it. To make matters worse she accidentally kicked him as she recrossed her long legs.

"I'm so sorry!" she exclaimed at once. He said nothing but went suddenly very pale and his eyes darkened. She saw him take a long swallow of his whisky, then give a rather wan little smile. "Are you all right?"

"Of course — it's just that you do have rather sharp heels!" He changed the subject abruptly. "How are you getting on at the Foundation?"

"I thought you weren't interested."

"I never said that; I said I wasn't involved; there is a difference, you know."

With a certain amount of care she told him something of her work, being very circumspect about Mrs Sinclair's attitude but praising the wonderful facilities that the Foundation provided.

"Are you finding it worthwhile then?"

"Oh yes, and exhausting; any new job can be tiring but when it involves thirty or so strange children . . . well, I leave you to imagine! You must come and see for yourself one day — when I'm a bit more organized." In the way she had come to recognize he appeared to lose interest.

"Perhaps . . . but you could come and see where we work." He leaned forward and spoke to Tom. "You've got to go in to the yard tomorrow, haven't you? And I've got those designs to go over — Cressida would like to see where we build the boats." He turned back to her. "You would, wouldn't you?"

"It might be a good idea if you asked her first, then me," Tom laughed. "Now the poor girl will have to say 'yes'. Well, Cressida?"

"Yes, I'd like that very much."

"Right then, shall we say about eleven?"

"I think we ought to make a move if we're to get those take-aways on the way home," Julia suggested. Tom stood up to let Cressida out of the booth, she turned back and spoke to Mike: "Thanks for the sailing lesson." She was rewarded by the smile she loved. "Till tomorrow then." The two girls could be heard arguing the merits of fish and chips or Chinese all the way up the steps.

* * *

Much to her surprise, 'Blakeney & Sons, Boatbuilders' was not anywhere near the sea. Large wooden gates were arched over with wrought-iron and the name picked out in gold. Cressida opened the smaller door, inset, and stepped into the yard. To her left was a two-storey office block. A man was just coming out. "Mr Carteret's office?" she enquired.

He held the door open. "This way, first on the right."

The door he had indicated stood ajar. She pushed it further. "Can I come in?"

Mike was seated behind a very large desk. Then she saw that it was really a large hollow square made with tables and filing units; the fourth side was against the back wall and she could see a bubbling coffee-percolator and mugs on it: smiling, he half rose from his seat as she came in. "Do sit down," he indicated one of the chairs outside the square. "I'm glad you're punctual, I get very grouchy if I'm kept waiting for my coffee!" he joked, swivelling his chair round. "Milk but no sugar if I remember rightly." Cressida nodded, pleased that he had taken note of such a small thing. "Tom will be here soon — he can smell coffee a mile away." They both laughed.

"By the way, Julia has told me what happened to Tom's wife and about Lucy. It seems he never hid anything from her. Anyway, I'm glad he told her the truth early on, concealing things can often cause great unhappiness later, don't you think?" She could see the muscles in his jaw tighten but if he was going to say something, he was prevented by the arrival of Tom.

"Ah! I thought I smelt coffee. Hello, Cressida." Mike filled a huge mug, twice the size of theirs with The Boss written in red on it. He handed it to Tom who spooned in three sugars.

Mike made a face at her. "I know, disgusting isn't it — but he won't listen."

Tom asked. "Where did you leave your car? If it's out in the street; we'd better get it in before I show you round or you'll probably get a ticket." He gulped down the coffee. "Give me the keys and I'll go and get it."

"It's only a Mini, Tom, you'd never get into it — if you open the gates I'll drive her in." They went out together. She had been expecting Mike to show her round but Tom explained that the boat-building side was his concern. He showed her the boats under construction and the area set aside for the DIY brigade, an idea of Mike's for making some cash when things had been slack and which was now very successful. All the time she was wondering how the boats got into the water, at last she could contain herself no longer. "Where's the water, Tom? I can't see any anywhere."

Tom laughed his big rumbling laugh and pointed to the very far end of the yard. "Down there, there's a canal with wet and dry docks. Did you think we dragged them through the streets? Although the small ones can come in that way on trailers." When the tour was over Tom said, "I'll leave you with Mike now, I know he has things he wants to show you." He disappeared up the stairs. Cressida re-entered the office. Mike was sitting at the computer that occupied all of one side of the desk.

"If you grab one of those chairs and bring it in here, I shall be able to demonstrate some of the wonders of modern technology." Cressida lifted the chair over the narrow gap and squeezed through herself. When they were seated side by side he said, "This is some of the software I use for showing the clients possible lay-outs for their equipment." She watched, fascinated as he drew various parts of a boat on the VDU screen and then using an electronic 'mouse' turned them this way and that, zooming in to show details of particular areas. With just a click of the 'mouse' he could locate and relocate instruments to suit every wish of the client. He explained how he was responsible for supervising the fitting of the equipment into the boats and controlling the sea-trials.

"And now I'll show you what I do to entertain the visitors." The screen went blank and then what he called a 'menu' came up. He showed Cressida how she could then use the 'mouse' to draw anything she liked on the screen, using a wide palette of colours and any kind of line that took her fancy, filling in and rubbing out at will.

He watched her draw, after a bit of trial and error, a house with an out-of-proportion cat sitting on the roof. She pushed the 'mouse' over to him. He drew a smile on the cat's face, then she rubbed its body out leaving only the head; Mike erased that, leaving the smile suspended above the house. They both dissolved into laughter. Mike leant over and pressed another key. Suddenly in flashing letters, as large as the screen would hold, appeared the words 'May I Kiss You.' Underneath in smaller letters it said 'press "Y" for yes'. He saw a question in her eyes. "No, Cressida," he said. "I designed this part of the entertainment only for you."

She looked at the keyboard carefully and then deliberately laid her finger on the letter 'Y'. For a second before all her attention went elsewhere she could see the screen burst into a blaze of changing colours, then all she was aware of was Mike's hands on either side of her face and his mouth coming down onto hers.

At first the kiss was gentle, searching but already it lit a fire that burned deep within her. He held her close and she could feel the strength of his back muscles as her arms came round his body. His passion increased and she responded, twining her fingers in his thick bronze hair, wanting the world to stop but time to go on forever. Every doubt she had had was swept away in the torrent of emotion she poured into the embrace. And then without warning she could feel the strength and tenderness change. The power of his mouth on hers became a cruel demanding pressure, bruising and cutting. He held her now, not in an embrace of passion but one of bitter anger, his hands on her upper arms biting painfully into her flesh. Suddenly it was over, he pushed her away and spun his chair round violently. For a moment Cressida sat there stunned, her hand up to her throbbing mouth.

Without turning round he spoke, his voice ragged. "Go . . . please go, Cressida . . . and don't . . . " He got no further.

Cressida regained her voice and finished off the sentence for him . . . "Don't worry, I won't come back and I won't trouble you with my presence anywhere else either!" She picked up her bag and swept out of the office where she met Tom coming downstairs.

"You off then?"

"Yes," was all she could manage. Tom went to open the gates for her and she drove out without a backward glance; he could hear the tyres screaming as she turned the next corner.

He closed the gates thoughtfully wondering what he was going to find in the office, but Mike seemed to be busy working at the computer, he didn't look up. "I think I have just put an end to what might have developed into an awkward situation. If you don't mind,

Tom, I've got quite a bit of work to catch up on."

Tom was nearly fooled into thinking that everything was more or less all right till he caught sight of the VDU screen. The diagram that Mike claimed he was working on was both upside-down and back to front. He retreated to his own office leaving Mike to fight his own special battle. Well at least I can do something to stop it getting worse for him, he thought. He picked up the phone and dialled the cottage. "Now listen carefully Julia, there isn't much time before Cressida gets back . . . "

★ ★ ★

For a week the tide of Cressida's anger sustained her. Mike's total rejection of her; and the way he had achieved it, made her go hot and cold every time she thought about it. She couldn't bring herself to tell Julia what had happened, merely saying that she and

Mike would no longer be seeing each other. "I'm sorry, Cress, but perhaps it's for the best."

But Cressida knew it wasn't. What he had done began to fade and she still felt as strongly as ever about the things that had attracted her to him. By the end of the first week she was starting to look for excuses for his behaviour; after a fortnight she abandoned the pretence of rationality and just longed numbly to see him again. The pain had to be plastered over during the day but sleepless nights and private anguish painted their picture on her face.

The only thing that flourished was the cottage garden, restoring it little by little to its former glory was real balm to her troubled spirit. She made friends with the man who ran the village store who, being a keen gardener himself, offered to bring his heavy-duty lawn-mower and see what he could do to tame the grass. In the wall she had discovered an ivy-covered door leading out to a lane that ran at the back of the cottage, the hinges were stiff and rusty but still serviceable and she managed to restore the door to working order and give it several coats of dark-green paint.

Cressida went over all the things she might do so that she could see Mike again. Going back to the yard was definitely out. She plucked up courage to phone but only got an answering-machine, so she just hung up. There was no Michael Carteret in the phonebook. She bought a map and spent the whole of one evening driving round the countryside looking for the place where they had had their dinner; eventually she found it but although her pockets were stuffed with sugar-lumps, Horace was not there. It seemed like the last straw. Finally she accepted an invitation to go out and have a drink with Tom and Julia, hoping that she might find out something, and she did; during conversation Tom let it drop that Mike was sorting out some problems with a boat moored at an east-coast yachting marina.

Nearly four weeks went by. Returning from work she found a florist's box propped against the front door. It was the sort of thing that Julia was always getting. She picked it up and saw that a pencilled note had been pushed underneath. 'For Miss C. Maitland', it read; there was nothing else on it but the name of a florist in Seahaven. With trembling fingers she undid the ribbon on the long slim box; inside was a single crimson rose, the exact twin of the one Mike had given her when they had dined in the motorvan. She looked through the box and wrapping but there was no card or message of any kind. Surely Mike must have sent it, but if it was meant as an apology, it certainly couldn't be interpreted as an invitation either. Nevertheless Cressida slept better that night than she had for weeks.

As well as working in the garden she had been working very hard at the Foundation, spending a lot of time in the classrooms, getting to know the children. As a result some of her paperwork had fallen behind. In an effort to catch up she decided to go in on Saturday morning. It hadn't gone particularly well, images of Mike kept flooding into her mind and the facts and figures she was attempting to correlate for her first report seemed to be making no sense. Just as she was about to give up and go home there was a knock on her office door. "Come in." Mary Potter, one of the house mothers, was standing there, seemingly in great distress. Mary was one of Cressida's supporters, she believed whole-heartedly in the scheme. "Whatever's the matter, Mary?"

"It's Karen Ainslie's party dress. You know Emma Jones has asked her to her birthday tea tomorrow?" Cressida nodded, it was something she was very pleased about . . . "One of the boys came in just now and he had a cup of tea in his hand; he must have tripped or something; anyway . . . look!" She held the dress up and Cressida could see that there was a nasty dark stain all down the front. "I'm afraid it won't wash out, it needs dry-cleaning. Karen's that upset, crying and saying she won't go . . . I don't know what to do; I can't leave the house just now and when I saw your car I thought . . . "

"Yes of course, I'll see what I can do. I believe there's a 'two-hour cleaners' in Seahaven; if I hurry they might just get it done today."

The nearest car-park to the High Street was behind and below it. A Saturday afternoon was not the best time to find a space but she was lucky, someone was just pulling out. She slid the Mini in and dashed across to the pay-and-display unit. She fumbled through her purse for the right coins for the slot-meter. Suddenly a familiar voice said, "will this do?" She was standing right next to the Jag and Mike himself was leaning over its roof holding out a 50p piece. Her heart somersaulted, then almost trance-like she leant across and took the coin, he held onto it for a moment so that she was forced to look into his eyes; she saw only gentleness there. "I'm so sorry, Cressida . . . about what happened . . . I want to explain . . . Will you let me? . . . Can we go somewhere and talk? . . . Now?"

All the words she had spent her sleepless nights rehearsing just melted away. "Yes," she replied simply, "but there's something I must do first. How about the 'Copper Kettle' in about twenty minutes?" She mentioned a tea-room that she and Julia knew.

"Right . . . twenty minutes then . . . and thank you . . ."

She failed miserably to convince the manager of the dry-cleaners to take on a two-hour cleaning job on a Saturday afternoon and now she was still left with a problem; not expecting anything like this she had come out without either cheque-book or credit cards. She'd just have to ask Mike if he could lend her enough money so that she could buy Karen a new dress. Cressida couldn't help smiling to herself. One minute she believed she might never speak to him again, now she was about to borrow money from him!

She looked at her watch. Ten of the twenty minutes had already gone and now she must try and find a suitable dress for the little girl; hopefully she could match the size and colour with the damaged one. She was unfamiliar with Seahaven as a shopping-centre but her luck held; in the window of a children's shop she saw just what she wanted. Nearly another five minutes went by before the assistant was free. Cressida drew in her breath a bit when she heard the price. She left a five-pound deposit on it — nearly all the money she had on her — and then made a dash for the 'Copper Kettle', knowing she was already late. It would be awful if Mike had left, thinking that she had deliberately taken a dreadful sort of revenge.

The relief of seeing him sitting alone

at a table for two was immense. She threaded her way through the crowded restaurant and took the vacant chair. Her first plan of being friendly but cool vanished as soon as she saw him close to. He looked dreadful. His eyes were huge and darkly set into a face that was thinner than she remembered, its angles standing out more sharply and the lines more deeply etched. There was a greyness in his complexion that even his tan could not disguise. Her opening remark was a totally natural response to what she saw. "My God, Mike, you look terrible! What's wrong?"

He gave a little one-sided smile. "Oh, Cressida, Cressida . . . " At that moment a waitress came with the tea things; he said nothing more until they had all been unloaded and then . . . "I ordered you a teacake in case you were hungry, they're supposed to be quite good here . . . "

"Michael Carteret, if you don't stop nattering on about tea-cakes and tell me what's wrong I shall leave." She half rose from the chair.

Quickly he leaned forward, putting his hand on her arm, and said earnestly, "No, please don't do that. Pour the tea and I'll try to tell you."

"That's better!" She filled two cups and handed him one. He took a small bottle from his inside jacket pocket and shook two tablets onto his palm.

"Oh Mike, you're not well, are you?"

"That's only part of it I'm afraid; I don't think you're going to like what I have to say."

"Try me."

Mike swallowed both the tablets with one gulp of tea. "Please don't say anything till I've finished. God knows this is difficult enough as it is." He drew in a deep breath and let it out slowly. He was not looking at her as he spoke, and his voice dropped almost to a whisper: "Several years ago I was in an accident . . . a bad one . . . and now I can't walk, well not very far, without the aid of crutches . . . I'm afraid I set out right from the beginning to deceive you, and I used Tom and Julia as conspirators in the plot too. It was wrong and stupid of me . . . I can only say I'm sorry."

Cressida's mind whirled and then, like a fruit machine delivering the jackpot, all the previously unexplained incidents fell into place. But there were also flashing danger-signals, by saying the wrong thing now she could surely wreck any future they might have. At that moment her love for him deepened into something that she knew would last all her life, and yet the relationship had never been more fragile.

The afternoon sun coming through the window struck gold into his bronze hair. Michael Carteret was offering her his broken sword. She must accept it with grace and wisdom. Then she knew, as if by instinct, what mattered most at that moment. She put her hand out so that it lay within reach of his and said, "Does it always hurt so much?

The truth please, Mike."

He looked up, smiled, and just for a moment laid his hand over hers, then withdrew it. "Like hell at the moment; anyway that's mostly my own fault, I was determined to get here without using crutches."

"I don't understand . . . why?"

"I'm not sure that I do myself, false pride, self-deception, bloody-mindedness or sheer stupidity perhaps because now I'm going to have to ask for your help to get back. I'm afraid there's no way I can walk that distance again."

Cressida tried to push all the implications of what he had told her to the back of her mind. The immediate problem was more important. "What do you want me to do?"

"Go back to my car and bring the crutches back here, then I can manage."

She studied him carefully; the tablets must be beginning to take effect because the pallor had gone. "Could you get into the Mini, do you think? It might be better if I brought it here, then I could drive you back to the Jag." She could see him measuring up the distance from the table to the door . . . "If you give me your keys, I'll bring the crutches too."

"You're very observant . . . and kind," he added. "Yes I'll accept the offer of the Mini, when the time comes. We've still got our tea to finish; you haven't touched your teacake and I expect you think you deserve some answers."

Cressida stirred her tea thoughtfully. "Mmm . . . but only one for the moment, Mike. Why? . . . Why did you feel you had to deceive me? I'm not a monster, you know. I wouldn't have refused to speak to you . . . or go out with you for that matter, just because you use crutches . . . "

"My dear girl, let me explain . . . in the beginning it had nothing whatsoever to do with you personally. It all started weeks ago in the pub. I think we were discussing things we would most like in life, you know the sort of thing. I must have had too much to drink because in an unguarded moment I said I would like to meet someone, just once more, who didn't think of me as a cripple first and a person second." Cressida gave a little gasp at the word cripple but his look defied interruption. "To be frank I didn't really mean 'someone', I meant a girl.

"Tom seemed to think it could be managed somehow . . . he must have been drunk too! Then he roped in Julia and as you were due to arrive in a few days you became the guinea-pig so to speak. I admit to having had doubts about it being fair to you, but as they pointed out it was only for one evening and in fact you need never know that a deliberate deception had been practised at all!" His voice was bitter. "It must seem so childish to you . . ."

"Go on." She couldn't trust herself to say more; her throat was constricted as she imagined the full meaning of his words: "just for once I wanted someone to see the man before they saw the cripple."

"Once I'd started I didn't want to stop. The hilltop dinner, the sailing trip, they made me feel marvellous, but by then Julia was getting quite annoyed about the whole thing and threatened to tell you herself. In the end I made a thorough mess of everything."

"Just how personal did it get? In the end, I mean?"

"Enough to make me wish that it had never begun with deception, and I'm afraid I got very angry . . . Oh, not with you," he added quickly, "with myself."

A little bleakly Cressida understood, that although there had been desire and finally frustration in their only kiss, there had not necessarily been any love. "I must say I think you were wrong not to tell me . . . that day in the office . . . instead of putting ridiculous messages up on the computer . . . "

Much to her surprise he started to laugh.

"You're fantastic, Cressida. I was so afraid of telling you, dreading that look of pity, or worse — fear, that comes into the eyes of so many when they first meet a disabled person. But you — you just tick me off! I think we ought to make a fresh start, don't you?"

"If that is what you want."

"Yes, very much." The expression in his eyes told her he was telling the truth.

Mike offered his hand. "Shake," he said, solemnly, sealing their pact of friendship.

"As one friend to another then, I'm going to have to ask you a favour . . . to do something for me." From the lift of his eyebrow and the wry smile, Cressida guessed that he was pleased not to be on the receiving end for once. "Do you think you could possibly lend me some money? I know one shouldn't ask . . . on such a short acquaintance," she added mischievously, "but I really am desperate."

"How much? . . . fifty pounds, a hundred?" He took out his wallet and started riffling through the notes.

"Stupid, twelve would cover it easily. It's for . . . "

"You don't have to tell me."

"I know but I want to." She went on to describe the events that had brought her into Seahaven.

"And you're planning to buy this dress out of your own money, I suppose?"

"Out of yours, actually, until I can pay you back."

"Let it be out of mine, Cressida. God knows I do very little for the Foundation, I usually find excuses not to go to the trustee meetings even."

She was about to remonstrate when she realized that that was the last thing she should do. "OK then, your twelve, my fiver. How's that?" Mike nodded and smiled as he handed over a ten and a five. "I'd better go now. If you give me your keys I can get your crutches and bring them back in the Mini, but I must buy that dress first. I won't be long; just time for you to eat that tea-cake!"

5

MIKE watched her leave the cafe. Long after she had disappeared he continued staring blindly out of the window, vowing then and there that never, under any circumstances, would he let her know how much she had come to mean to him. But surely it couldn't be wrong to keep her friendship?

Cressida tried to organize her thoughts, so much had happened so quickly. For the moment she just prayed that she had handled the situation successfully so far. Now that she knew Mike was disabled, she couldn't imagine how stupid she'd been not to realize something of the sort sooner. All the clues, however cleverly disguised, had been there and she had seen none of them.

She looked at the keys Mike had

given her and noticed they were attached to an unusual key-ring — a deep-blue enamel disc with his monogram in silver — and saw that they both had the same initials — only reversed.

She found the crutches lying behind the front seats, they were of the elbow type with hinged cuffs, rather battered and lighter than she expected. She could see now that the Jag was an automatic one, modified so that the brake and accelerator pedals could be used by the left foot.

As she drove back she tried to sort out her feelings and imagine what his might be. For certain hers had not altered, but Mike? That was altogether different. He wanted a friend, one who wouldn't pity him or be afraid of his disability . . . well, she would just have to be that sort of friend — love would have to wait.

Once back at the cafe people at several tables looked curiously as she went by carrying the crutches; she handed them to Mike.

"I've paid the bill. Did you get the dress all right?" He fitted the cuffs of the crutches over his forearms as he spoke.

She walked ahead of him so that she could hold the door open. "The passenger side is unlocked . . . if you . . . " she let the suggestion hang in the air.

"Yes, I think I can." He matched the action to the words by putting both crutches in one hand and opening the door. "It is rather a long way down," he said a little ruefully, glancing at the seat.

"Do you want any help?"

"Please." He put his hand on her shoulder and lowered himself into the car, a sudden tightening of the grip telling her it must still be hurting. She handed in the crutches. When she was settled in the driving-seat he said, "I don't want you to think I'm always as bad as this but recently I've been having a bit of trouble with my right leg, that's the worst one . . . I think

I may have damaged it in one of the boats the other day . . . "

"So you thought you'd give it a real work-out by walking all that way without your crutches. The next thing I know you'll be tripping over your stiff upper lip!" Her little joke was rewarded by a look of real appreciation.

"In order to celebrate our reacquaintance, will you come to supper with me — tonight, at my house?"

"Before I accept there is one thing that I want to clear up . . . "

"And that is?" he queried.

"If we are going to see more of each other I don't want to make a nuisance of myself by asking: Can you do this? Are you all right? Can I help you? You must know the sort of thing I mean. I want you to promise me that you will tell me the truth, that if you're tired, or in pain or can't manage something or need help, you will say so. In return I promise not to pester you with any of those questions."

There was a moment's silence, then,

"I promise . . . now will you come to supper with me?"

"Gladly, if you tell me where you live!"

"It's called Summerfield Place, you'll find it on the map . . . I presume you did buy one eventually?"

"Yes I did, an Ordnance Survey, so no problem." Not for the world would she admit the real reason for her purchase of the map. As she handed over the keys of the Jag he asked her to get there about seven.

Cressida delivered the new dress to Mary Potter and saw the delighted look on little Karen's face, at least that story might well have a happy ending. Now she could hardly wait to get back to the cottage and tell her sister what had happened. She burst through the front door. "Julia, are you there? Juliaaa!"

"In the bathroom," came the muffled reply, "washing my hair." Cressida took the stairs two at a time, and not waiting till her sister emerged she thrust open the bathroom door. "Oh

111

Julia! I've seen Mike again . . . I know about his legs . . . you might have told me . . ."

Julia wrapped her hair in a turban. "I didn't tell you any lies, you know." She leant forward and looked in the mirror to smooth out her eyebrows. "I only withheld some of the truth."

"Rather a large chunk of it; if you ask me! I went through hell after Mike and I broke up, couldn't you have said something then?"

"I probably would have if Tom hadn't phoned up while you were on your way back from the yard that day, and made me promise not to."

"Why should he do that?"

"It seems he figured that if you learnt the whole truth then, you might have rushed straight back, full of pity and remorse, and that would have been disastrous for Mike."

Cressida gave this reasoning some thought — there was certainly more than a grain of truth in it. She conceded that Tom was right to have protected

112

his friend. "What do you know about the accident that caused his injuries?"

"Very little, I'm afraid. I think it was about five years ago, not long after Tom's wife died in fact, but neither of them talk about it." Julia started to comb out her hair.

"What do you know about Summerfield Place then?" Cressida tried again.

"Absolutely nothing — look, sis, I am tired of telling you how little I know and although you're infatuated with this guy, I just can't see you being happy with someone who isn't able to share the sort of things you like . . . you know . . . walking . . . skiing . . . etc."

"Oh yeah," replied her sister, stung to anger, "and how much interest has Tom got in the theatre then?"

"Don't be silly, Cress! That's different."

"Anyway Mike and I have just agreed to be friends again, that's all, and I'll settle for that . . . for the time being at least."

"Humph," was the only reply her sister gave.

Summerfield Place was as easy to find as Mike said it would be and by five to seven Cressida found herself approaching a magnificent pair of wrought-iron gates, she was about to stop the car when they began to swing open of their own accord. They were the first of many electronic systems that Mike had installed to assist in maintaining his independence. Through the mature trees that lined the drive she could see the gleam of water, rounding the final curve revealed the full beauty of a lawn sweeping gently down to a little reed-fringed lake.

The drive widened out into a semicircle, on the straight side of which stood a charming Queen Anne manor house. Beyond it was a paddock with more trees and surely that was Horace contentedly grazing in the lush summer grass. Somehow the place seemed familiar and yet Cressida knew she had never been there before; then in the distance she saw a steeply wooded hillside. In her mind's eye she recalled the valley Mike had shown her on their first date; no wonder he said he loved it — he had been showing her his own home! She was about to put her hand on the brass lion-head knocker, when that door too swung open. Mike was standing in the hallway, a broad grin on his face. "You found it all right then?"

"Why didn't you tell me? Why be so secretive . . . ?"

"Tell you what?" he replied innocently.

"You know perfectly well what I mean, that it was this house we were looking at that evening."

"I just wanted you to enjoy the beauty of the valley for its own sake."

"I hope you don't think it would have made any difference if I'd known that you were master of all you surveyed!"

"Well I'm not, not exactly," he said wryly. "I'll tell you about it later. Meanwhile come on in." He ushered her into a large room with a high moulded ceiling, white panelled walls and a carved marble fireplace. It was furnished with a suite of furniture in plain coral-coloured covers. On one side of the fireplace was a leather reclining-chair and between two windows, a dining-table. The occasional tables, cabinets and the gilded mirror over the mantelpiece were genuine antiques and the walls were hung with original oils. "Wow!" was all she could think of to say, and a subdued "Yes, please" when he offered her a drink.

He sat in the leather chair and swung a small table across in front of him, then he opened a cupboard and took out two glasses. "What would you like?" He offered a variety of apèritifs. Cressida chose a medium sherry. "You'll have to come over and collect it, I'm afraid, carrying things is not one of my strong points." He gave her a penetrating look. "You're very quiet — that's not like you; I don't embarrass you now, do I?"

"Of course not, it's not you . . . it's this place. I feel quite overwhelmed, I suppose it's sort of confused me about the kind of person you are . . . I'd thought of you as being someone who works for a living . . . not part of the landed gentry . . . but then your name is Carteret, so perhaps I should have known . . . " Her voice tailed off.

"There's no need for that. None of this," he gestured towards the grounds and the lake, glinting in the late evening sunshine, "is quite what it seems. Would you like to hear about it?" She nodded. "My great-great-grandfather," Mike pointed to one of the portraits, "built 'Sandilands', where you now work. His son made even more money and left it to my grandfather, who then quarrelled with my father and disinherited him, setting up the Carteret Foundation instead. Only this house and the land surrounding it were to remain in family hands and then only if there is a Carteret to live in it. When I'm gone, it too will revert to the Foundation."

"Oh but you could marry and have children and then there'd be Carterets to go on living here . . . " Cressida spoke without thinking and then stopped abruptly, seeing the bleak look in his eyes.

"You think so, do you?"

She made her voice casual. "I expect you just haven't met the right girl yet, that's all. Do you resent what your grandfather did?"

Mike held out his hand to take her glass for a refill. "Sometimes, but it all happened before I was born. It was quite different for my father though, not that he was left entirely penniless. He died when I was five, but I hardly remember him, he spent a lot of time abroad. So although I live in such a beautiful house, I certainly have to work hard to keep us both!"

"And your mother, is she . . . ?"

"Very much so . . . she married again some years ago . . . a genuine millionaire this time, they live in

California. I also have a sister who lives in Australia with her husband and two children. So you see I am positively surrounded by relatives!"

Cressida was determined to probe a little further. "Don't you get lonely though, shut away behind those great iron gates?"

"I don't think of myself as shut away, there's Tom and the clients and I have my housekeeper." His reply was rough and she realized that perhaps she had touched a raw nerve, but before she could retract a little he said, "I think we'd better eat now."

She could see that the table was laid for two and that an electric hostess-trolley was plugged in nearby. Mike put his hand out to pick up the crutches leaning against his chair. She made up her mind quickly. "Would it be breaking any promises if we eat here?" Before waiting for an answer she went on, "I'll bring the trolley over and I can use this." She pointed to the coffee-table in front of the sofa.

Mike gave her a long, searching look and she could feel that his will-power and the pain were fighting a battle. At last he relaxed and his eyes smiled. "No," he answered, his tone grateful, "in this instance I'll waive the promise."

Cressida immediately set about serving the food, which was plain but appetizing. When it was finished she did not linger, guessing him to be very tired but allowing him to see her out to the car. Promises were promises after all. Before getting in she hesitated. "Are you very busy tomorrow? Tom and Julia are taking Andrew to the zoo, so I shall be on my own . . . if you like you could come over and try my style of cooking."

Her question was followed by a very long silence. Was he hunting for a polite way of saying 'no'? Then the memory of something Julia had once nearly said came back and she realized that the two flights of steep steps up to the cottage might present him with

120

an almost insurmountable difficulty. The silence was broken by two voices speaking at once. Mike said, "I'm sorry but I don't think I can manage those steps just now." And Cressida said, "You won't have to use the steps because I've found a door in the wall that leads into a lane . . . "

Mike shook his head. "I might have guessed you d come up with a solution. OK, I accept. Anyway we've already eaten my Sunday lunch!"

* * *

She showed him where to leave his car, close to her newly-discovered door. "I'd no idea that this was here," she said, "until I got the rubbish cleared away and cut back some of the ivy." She led the way down the path towards the revived lawn with its spreading fruit-tree, now showing a scattering of baby apples. Beneath it she had set out the expensive garden furniture that Julia had bought and put a tray of drinks and glasses on the table. "It's such a lovely day I thought we'd have our lunch out here. I'm afraid it's a cold one anyway, I hope you don't mind?"

"Of course not, it's not really roast and two veg weather. Before I sit down I'd like to have a look round your garden. I just can't believe this is the same place I saw only a few months ago."

Cressida was pleased that he appreciated her efforts. "OK then, and when you've had enough, there's a bottle of wine to be opened and help yourself to a drink."

She went in and from the kitchen window she watched him move about on his crutches, the first time she had been able to do this without him knowing. At once she could see that he put less weight on his right leg, using it to balance as he pushed off and landed on the left one. The damage to it had obviously been very severe. She wondered how it had happened; she certainly wasn't going to ask, perhaps he would soon have enough confidence in their friendship to tell her. She carried out the tray with two plates of cold meat, a bowl of mixed salad and a jug of her own home-made dressing. She had spent some of the morning making wholemeal Irish soda-bread to eat with slightly salted butter. After the meal, under the influence of the wine and in the dappled shade of the tree, Mike finally dozed off.

Cressida took herself off to the far side of the garden and began weeding. When he woke Mike kept quiet, watching her work, crouched intently over the bed. At last she sat back and surveyed the progress so far.

He felt like an avid collector at a museum, looking longingly at a unique object that he would never be able to possess. He didn't know which was the stronger feeling; the pleasure or the pain. The very real pain in his leg caused him to shift in the chair. He knew that he could no longer put off a visit to his doctor; he sighed. God knew he had had enough of the medical profession.

Cressida heard the movement and the sigh; she stood up and came towards him. He still looked tense and drawn, even after the sleep. She knew she could help him to relax, using techniques she had learned in college, but should she? Would he consider it a breach of their pact? As casually as possible she put a hand on his shoulder and keeping her voice neutral said, "You're a bit tensed up. May I do something about it?"

"If you like," was the rather gruff reply. She began by gently moving her fingers in a circular motion on his forehead, working her way slowly down past his temples and round to the back of his neck. When she reached his shoulders she could feel the immense power of them, the result of taking his weight on crutches; as she worked on them with the pressure of her fingers she could feel him relaxing. She would have gone on to work on his chest muscles, where she could see a bronze T of hair under his unbuttoned shirt. Suddenly he put an arm up behind her head and pulled her face down towards his. She felt his cheek against hers, but what he would have done next she would never find out — at that moment a little misshapen apple fell with a plop onto his chest. He released her immediately and held it up — "forbidden fruit indeed" — the ironic laugh that accompanied his words was totally devoid of humour.

"I'll go and make some tea," Cressida said, glad of an excuse to escape.

* * *

Mike arrived late for work on Monday morning; "I may have to have some days off in the near future. Will you be able to cope?"

Tom looked thoughtfully at him. "What's up then?"

"I've been to see the doctor; he wants me to have some X-rays done and I may have to go up to Boroughfield and see old Ponting." Mike mentioned the hospital and the orthopaedic surgeon who had been in charge after the accident. "But I don't want you saying anything . . . to anyone, you understand?"

"Perfectly . . . Julia tells me you've seen Cressida again." For all Mike's physical and mental toughness — and Tom had experienced both; as an unfailing support after his own wife died and in taking a full share of the work when they had sailed, double-handed to Australia — looking at him now, Tom saw a vulnerability that had never been there before. Back in his office, he wondered what he could do to help. He lifted the phone. "Mike, I want you to take the rest of the week off and if you say 'no' I'll make it an order." There was a moment's silence at the other end then, "All right Tom . . . and thanks."

Tom was staggered, he had never expected such instant surrender; now he was really worried, Mike must be feeling much worse than he was letting on, but his next words were more reassuring.

"By the way it's the Yacht Club Ball on Wednesday night, have you got a partner for Cressida?"

"No, because she's resisted all attempts by me and Julia to get her to come." Tom was about to ask him if he felt fit enough but then thought better of it; instead he said. "It's half-term at the nursery school this week, so you'll probably catch her at the cottage. Go on home now."

Tom didn't resume his work for a few minutes, thinking of Mike. He knew that any trouble with the right leg was bad news, it could mean life in a wheelchair; he knew it was Mike's great fear, not that he ever spoke about it much. He had once said half humorously that crutches had their drawbacks — try using a self-service restaurant or going through revolving doors! He had stopped thinking of Mike as disabled, but had he made too many demands on a man who would go to any lengths not to show weakness? If Anna had been alive she would have seen what had been happening. Christ, he'd become thoughtless and selfish, but surely it was Cressida who was responsible for destroying Mike's peace of mind. He wished now he hadn't said anything about half-term.

Mike was on the phone as soon as he got home. "I've got some time off. Would you like to come over, if you're not doing anything with Julia, that is?"

"Didn't Tom tell you, she's away, but coming back on Wednesday, in time for the Yacht Club 'do'."

"Tom tells me you won't go. Could I persuade you to change your mind?"

There was nothing Cressida would have liked better than to be Mike's partner at the ball. "You might . . . but isn't it too late . . . I mean, aren't all the places taken by now?"

"Don't worry about it, that'll be

no problem. All you have to do is say yes."

"In that case, yes, I'd love to."

"Good. Now how about my first question?"

"I'm sorry, what was it?"

He gave a little sigh and repeated, "Would you like to come over this afternoon and bring your swimming-gear." This time she accepted gladly.

After Mike's call the half-term week took on a different aspect — if he was not working either, surely they could be together, getting to know one another better . . . Oh don't lie to yourself, she chided, what you really mean is that you want him to make love to you. But as she approached the closed iron gates of Summerfield Place she recognized that her love must be equally firmly contained, at least until the day Mike wanted to open the gates of her heart for himself.

She could see him standing by the paddock fence. He was patting Horace and fondling his ears. The sugar-lumps

Cressida had taken on her attempt to find the horse were still in the glove compartment, so she grabbed a few and went over to join them. "May I give him some sugar?"

Mike was running his hand along the glossy chestnut coat and Cressida guessed that the horse had once been his own, which he could no longer ride.

"Well, we've got other things to do. Did you bring a swim-suit like I said?"

Cressida nodded but was a bit puzzled; surely the lake was too cold? She collected her gear from the car. Mike took her through a door in a wall that extended out from the house, it led into a luxurious covered swimming-pool. "Fantastic!" She exclaimed, rushing forward and scooping up the warm water with her hand.

Mike just smiled. "You'll find a changing-room at the other end." By the time she emerged, clad in a black one-piece that showed off her athletic figure, Mike was already in the pool, pulling from one end to the other in a rhythmical front crawl. He turned on his back and whistled appreciatively. "Don't just stand there, c'mon in. You said you could swim." She ran round to the far end and dived neatly in, surfacing about halfway along. Mike was beside her. "Nice dive, let's go!" They set off together and at first she was able to keep up with him, but after about ten lengths her arms began to ache and she felt herself getting short of breath. She swam to the side and held on, panting; he ploughed up and down a couple more times then joined her.

"I'm not as fit as I thought I was," she admitted, getting her breath back. "How often do you do this?"

"Twice a day usually, before work and when I get back in the evening, fifty to a hundred lengths each time."

"Wow! That's incredible!"

"There's no need to be so bloody patronizing Cressida, it's the only way

I can keep fit." His eyes blazed.

Cressida felt as if he had slapped her in the face and she wasn't going to stay and find out why. She levered herself out of the water and went to the changing-room without a backward glance. By the time she was dressed again the pool was empty and the crutches that had been lying on the side had gone.

6

THE end of the pool-house had a wide area with some chairs and a small table. Cressida swept past it — still angry that Mike should have taken her genuine admiration as an insult, but also angry with herself for reacting too quickly, it was what her father had warned her against.

Her bag caught on the edge of the table and spilt its pile of yachting magazines onto the floor. With a muttered 'damn', she began to pick them up. The cover of one of them suddenly caught her eye. There, in glorious colour, were Tom and Mike, posed in front of a smallish yacht. There was a flash across one corner with the words: 'Handicapped sailor reaches Perth, see page 12'. She sat down, her anger forgotten, and turned eagerly to that page. There was the full story of the expedition to Australia. Cressida was so absorbed that she didn't notice Mike come in, and she jumped as he spoke. "I always thought the caption on the cover was a bit unfair on poor old Tom, after all, he looks perfectly sane to me!"

"Am I allowed to say what a terrific effort I think this was, without getting slapped down again?"

"Yes . . . I deserved that . . . I suppose one builds a sort of defence against praise, especially for physical things, it can so often be merely condescending." His words hit home. She was only just beginning to understand what it cost him to defend his independence. He went on, "Is there anything else you'd like to do?"

He looked tired but nothing would induce her to say so. "Sit down and have a cup of tea perhaps?"

"Good idea." Mike showed her into a room she hadn't seen before. "This is my office-cum-studio."

She could see all the usual

appurtenances of an office including another computer. There was also a separate table with paints, brushes and a stack of paper, but none of this was what gave the room its impact. The walls were quite literally covered with small water-colour paintings in gilded frames. Mostly, the subjects were botanical. It was like walking into a garden. Mike stood back as she walked round the room looking at each one in turn and all of them signed in minute letters M. Carteret. Cressida was speechless. Into the silence he dropped the words, "You can praise these as much as you like, I don't have to use my legs to do them!"

Without taking her eyes away from the pictures she said firmly, "Don't tease." The last half-hour had taught her a lot. "I do think they're wonderful though. You're too damned talented for me!" He was sitting down now watching her as she examined each one. "Have you always been keen on painting?"

"Not really. I was in hospital for a long time and fairly immobile for a lot of it. The OTs got pretty desperate trying to find something for me to do. One of them brought some paint and paper and I just started on the first thing to hand, which was a vase of flowers left on my locker. It all took off from that and now I sell almost everything I do. Would you like to have one?"

"Wouldn't I just! You choose one for me, Mike?"

He thought for a moment. "I know you like garden flowers but I think a wild flower would suit you better . . . a rare and beautiful one." She gave him a quick glance but he was quite serious, "There, that one over there," he pointed to a bold, purple bell-shaped bloom, its head delicately poised on a slender green stem ringed with fluffy leaves. 'The Pasque Flower' . . . do you like it? Go on, take it off the wall."

"It'll leave a gap."

"Every time I see it I'll think of you," he replied.

She cradled the little frame in her hands. "That's a poor exchange for this." Impulsively she went forward and kissed him on the cheek. He turned away immediately.

"Think nothing of it," he said tightly.

Sensing his anger she burst out: "For goodness sake! I thought we agreed to be friends. You gave me a present. I thanked you in the way friends often do. What's wrong with that?"

He didn't answer the question but said rather brusquely, "If you want that cup of tea you'll find everything in the kitchen . . . through that door."

As she waited for the kettle to boil her mind was totally given over to the man in the next room who she was sure was suffering not only physical pain but also the loneliness of having no one he could trust with his feelings. Cressida's pain was knowing that she could do nothing.

Mike waited for her to return, still

feeling the sensation of her kiss; her lightest touch nearly sent him into orbit — if he wasn't careful all his meticulously built defences would disintegrate; even now they seemed to be giving at the edges. Then the vision of himself as a grovelling, self-pitying heap put the iron back into his soul and by the time she reappeared with a tray he was in control again.

* * *

Mike was relieved when the session at the X-ray department was over and he could enjoy Cressida's company for a little while. He'd told her that he'd had some business to clear up and left his arrival-time open. It was yet another lie but he convinced himself it was justifiable; friendship had its limits.

He entered by her green door, expecting to find her working in the garden. Then through the open French windows he could see her sitting cross-legged on the floor; she was wearing jeans and a T-shirt, her hair done up in a high pony-tail. All around were rolls of white paper and she was drawing with a thick, red marker-pen. "What on earth are you doing? Making your own wallpaper?"

"Something like that; if you can pick your way through this mess I'll try and explain. It all seemed such a good idea at the time, now I'm not at all sure. It was meant to be a sort of mural for the large classroom; I thought I could cheer it up without actually painting on the wall itself."

Mike had perched himself on the arm of one of the chairs. "My dear girl — if I may say so, you will never do any good with those materials, the paper's too thin and the colours aren't bright enough. What sort of design had you in mind anyway?"

"I started out with all sorts of ideas; at their most ambitious I thought of a sort of continuous landscape effect with various characters going about their traditional business — you know the sort of thing? Bo-Peep, Red Riding Hood, Goldilocks . . . "

"An all-female society, I see!"

"Not at all, I also had in mind that thieving Tom the Piper's son and that lazy Boy Blue!" she retorted, entering into the spirit of the thing. "But I fear that my 'vaulting ambition' has indeed 'o'erleapt itself', so I'm now thinking more in term of coloured stripes and squiggles!"

"I have two questions. One, why can't you ask the Foundation to co-operate in this seemingly laudable venture, and two: would you consider leaving this with me to see what I can do?"

Cressida doodled on the paper before answering. "If I give you a truthful answer to question one, I don't want you to think that I'm whingeing. Whatever problems I have in my job are for me to solve. But I can tell you that I'm not exactly flavour of the month at the Foundation and to be perfectly honest I don't want to make any request that might rock the boat. On the other hand the classrooms are my concern and if I want them decorated, they damn well will be, even if I have to do it myself, which I am — I mean I'm trying to. As to question two, the answer is 'no'. It would be quite wrong for you to ring up and say," here she put on a deep pompous voice, "This is Trustee Carteret; I order you to do anything Miss Maitland demands!" They both laughed.

"I wouldn't do anything like that — but without anyone knowing I just might be able to exert a little pressure. However I won't, unless you say so. Incidentally, have you got the measurements of what you want?"

Cressida crawled over the floor, looking under bits of paper; at last she found a tatty-looking envelope. "There they are." She handed it to Mike who tucked it away in his inside blazer pocket. She saw he was wearing a crisp white shirt and a silk tie, presumably because of the business meeting he had mentioned. His legs were encased in well-cut beige slacks but there was something different; from the heel of his right shoe she could see what looked like two metal splints . . . he noticed the direction of her gaze.

"It's a caliper, designed to take the weight off the lower leg. The brace I normally use is invisible to the outsider, but this thing," he tapped it, "gives a bit of extra clout when . . . " he hesitated . . . "when required."

"Oh." Then feeling she ought to say something else Cressida added, "Is it very uncomfortable?" Then wished she hadn't.

"It does its job," he replied laconically. "One can't expect perfection when one's leg has been broken in twenty-seven places!"

Cressida looked at him stunned, but his expression didn't invite questions, so instead she said, "There's no answer to that, is there? I think I'll go and make some sandwiches — I'm starving. How about you?"

He let out a bellow of laughter. "You, Cressida Maitland, are the best thing that's happened to me." As she left the room she thought, if only I could believe that.

★ ★ ★

From Cressida's point of view the Yacht Club Ball was something of a disappointment. She had taken immense pains with her appearance and even remembered to wear the expensive perfume, all in the hope of evincing Mike's approval, but although he purported to be her escort his attentions fell far short of her expectations. In fact he seemed determined to deny that he was 'with' her at all, allowing Tom and Julia to bring her and take her home. He turned out to be the life and soul of the party, there were a couple of spare chairs tactfully placed beside his, and a whole host of people came and spoke to him, but throughout the evening he hardly paid any more attention to her than he did to others and he kept finding partners for her to dance with. She felt hurt and in a funny sort of way, jealous. She was also a little worried, there was an almost feverish quality to his high spirits which could not be accounted for by the small amount he drank. On her return from dancing with an incredibly boring man, she found that he had gone, inexplicably he had left the party without a word to her.

"He asked me to give you this." Tom handed her a folded note. Inside were the words. 'The Smugglers' 7.30 tomorrow, please.' It was just signed 'M'. All evening Cressida had the feeling that Mike was trying to underline the limitations his disability imposed. As a method of putting her off it was a failure; now that he had gone the party was over for her too.

★ ★ ★

The next day was hot and humid, the sun seemed to devour the air leaving

144

it breathless. Cressida was finding it impossible to concentrate on the clothes Julia was selecting; she finally lost patience. "Look here, Cressida, I only came up to town today because you said you wanted my help and you're not co-operating one bit."

"I'm sorry, Ju. My mind's just not on it. Perhaps it's the weather."

"Perhaps nothing," her sister retorted. "Your mind is back in a certain house in Sussex, or rather on the owner of it, am I not right?"

"I suppose so," Cressida sighed. "I'd really like to talk to you about it; let's go and find a coffee, perhaps I'll feel more like shopping afterwards."

The department store restaurant was air-conditioned so at least that made the heat more bearable. "I'm listening," said Julia, once they were seated.

"Actually I don't think there's really much to say. It all comes down to one simple fact. I am very much in love with a man who doesn't love me. End of story."

"How do you know?"

"How do I know what? That I love him or that he doesn't love me?"

"Both."

"OK, here goes then. He's in my thoughts night and day. He is the most attractive, sexually desirable man I have ever known. He is also kind, generous, amusing, talented and courageous beyond belief. I want to sleep with him, have his children and marry him — in any order you care to put it! Well you know what I mean! Does that satisfy you on the first count?"

"Now why do you believe he doesn't love you?"

"That's a little more difficult to answer. He accepts my friendship but even the slightest show of affection has him running a mile. Every time I make the tiniest move towards him emotionally he either slaps me down or runs away from it! I don't think I can take much more of it, Julia, and I just don't know what to do." Cressida's eyes filled with unaccustomed tears, she dashed them away with the back of her hand and blew noisily into her paper table-napkin. "I'm sorry, Ju," she gave a wan little smile, "this isn't like me at all."

"I'll tell you what I think. You say he 'runs away' every time you try to get closer to him. Has it ever occurred to you that it is the very fact that he can't run at all that makes him so distant?"

"You're trying to make out that he really does love me but won't say so because he's crippled, his word not mine incidentally, is that it?"

"In a nutshell, yes."

"No!" Cressida was vehement. "If that's the case I don't believe he would want to see me at all, I think he would avoid me rather than seek out my company."

Julia shrugged her shoulders. "You may be the one with the sociology diploma, Cress, but you haven't had my experience with men. Even in this day and age they want to be the protectors, the dragon-slayers, when they're in love. Imagine how disadvantaged Mike must feel . . . "

"But I don't give a stuff about him being disabled," Cressida broke in.

"I know that, and you know that, but can Mike bring himself to believe it? . . . I don't think so — at least not yet. You'll just have to stick close and let time do its thing. I wouldn't give up hope if I were you. Tom says that Mike has the strongest willpower of any man he has ever known. If a man like that doesn't want you to know something, he's quite capable of keeping it to himself. Now, do you want to do some more shopping?"

"If you don't mind I think I'll give it a miss, Julia. We'd only start to argue again. I thought I might go to a movie or something . . . you could go home; take the Mini from the station if you like. I'm supposed to be meeting Mike at 'The Smugglers' later and you're seeing Tom there aren't you? So you can bring the car back for me then."

"You're sure you'll be OK, Cressy?"

"Of course . . . and thanks for listening to me and for your advice." The sisters embraced with genuine affection.

* * *

Doctor Howard opened the envelope and took out the X-ray plates, putting them one at a time onto his viewing screen. He tapped a thoughtful pencil on his desk as he read the radiologist's report, looked up Michael Carteret's phone number and started to dial. As he waited for an answer he kept his eyes on the plates. "Doctor Howard here, I've got your results through — I'm afraid it's not good news — well you were half expecting that, weren't you? I'm going to arrange for you to see your orthopaedic specialist as soon as possible — when I've done that I'll call and see you . . . meanwhile keep off that leg," the doctor warned.

Mike listened to all this in virtual

silence — most of his worst fears were being confirmed and the spectres that haunted the dark recesses of his mind took a step closer. All he said was, "Do what you think is best, doctor, I'll be here."

When he arrived, the doctor explained that Mike had developed an infection in the bone which had to be dealt with at once. "There will be a bed for you at Boroughfield tomorrow. Now how will you get there? You certainly mustn't drive yourself."

"I can arrange something." He knew Tom would take him. "But oh God, I wish I didn't have to go."

"I know," the Doctor's voice was full of kindness, "but you must, you really must." He dived into his bag and brought out two bottles. "These are the antibiotics that Mr Ponting wants you to start immediately, and the others are some pain killers, for the journey. Now have you any questions?"

"When you spoke to him did Mr Ponting say what he wanted to do?"

Mike tried to keep his voice casual but the doctor was well aware of the desperate anxiety behind it. At its worst he knew the answer might be to amputate, but things hadn't reached that stage yet. He equivocated. "The infection has got to be reduced and then he will do what he can to stabilize the bone . . . "

"And if he can't . . . ?"

"I shouldn't cross that bridge yet if I were you." Mike, who had had plenty of experience in reading between the medical profession's lines, said nothing. The spectre had taken another step forward.

After the doctor had gone, he tipped his reclining chair back and lay with his eyes closed. All the things he was facing now he had faced before and overcome, why then did it all seem so much worse now? The answer was in his heart, not his mind. For the first time he had found someone he wanted to share his life with. He desperately needed all the wonderful things she had to give but which a cruel fate forbade him to take. To stand alone now was doubly difficult. He made up his mind to tell Cressida that he was merely going to hospital for a routine checkup, no need for flowers or visits, especially as it was a long way away. He rehearsed the phrases till they seemed to come naturally. Then he phoned Tom, who agreed at once to drive him to Boroughfield next morning.

The storm-clouds that had been building up all afternoon finally rumbled into life with the first flash of lightning and then the rain began, big splatty drops that soaked into the dry earth and refreshed the air. Mike considered calling a cab to take him to 'The Smugglers' but changed his mind. Dr Howard be damned, he thought, and got into the Jag, revelling in its power and his ability to control it. That at least would still be left to him whatever else the future held.

The pub was fairly empty and his favourite booth was free. Cressida had not yet arrived which gave him more time to polish his well-thought-out speech. Then suddenly and unaccountably he wanted to change his mind — to confess his desperate need of her — to tell her that he was scared of, what the future might hold. He wanted to make love to her, to bury his fears in the strength of her body, to experience the love he was sure she was beginning to feel for him, and surrender to the tide of emotion dammed up within him . . . these thoughts, which were as refreshing as the rain had been to the parched earth, were halted as the drone of voices coming from the upper bar dissolved into one he was familiar with; there was no mistaking Julia's beautifully modulated tones.

He heard her say Cressida's name and then. "Of course she's ideally suited to the job. The . . . what's the modern buzz-word for it? . . . the disadvantaged . . . Yes, they just feed out of her hand. Show my sister a lame dog and it's over the stile before it knows it! And all in the most tactful way . . . " If she said anything else Mike did not hear it, what was left of his world had just collapsed in ruins.

7

MIKE'S attitude had thrown Cressida into a state of total confusion for the second time. Now her whole mind was occupied, trying to work out the reason for it. Everything that she had hoped to gain from her talk with Julia had been lost. Certainly she had kept him waiting but that was no fault of hers, the train had been delayed by flooding on the line, and she had arrived at 'The Smugglers' with wet hair and mud-splashed clothes. But Mike had never seemed to be the sort of man to whom these things mattered. He was in his favourite seat, but her smile of pleasure at seeing him had found no answering expression from him. She had sat down, apologizing for her appearance being both late and dishevelled. Mike had accepted her explanation without comment, merely asking her what she would like to drink, adding that it was 'good of her to bother to come at all in such weather'.

She noticed his eyes had a bleak, dead look and the spirited reply to his remark had died in her throat, unuttered. He was treating her like a stranger.

She had barely finished her drink when he ostentatiously looked at his watch and said. "Good heavens! Is that the time? I'm afraid you'll have to excuse me, I've been called away unexpectedly on business and there are a lot of things to do before I leave tomorrow."

Cressida had tried to find out where he was going and when he would be back but he was noncommittal, implying that he would be travelling around indefinitely. He eased himself out of the booth and she automatically tucked her legs out of his way. His final words, uttered without sincerity or emotion, chilled her to the bone. "I must thank you for giving up so much of your half-term holiday to entertaining me. It was very kind of you." She watched uncomprehendingly as he fitted his crutches and disappeared from the room, from the building, and with a deep inner despair she knew it was from her life too.

★ ★ ★

Their journey to Boroughfield started early. Tom found Mike looking ill, tired and drained in a way he'd never seen before. He sat in the passenger seat with his eyes closed for most of the way. North of London they stopped at a motorway service-station. "I'll find a table, just coffee for me please," Mike requested.

Tom plonked the tray down on the table, slopping the coffee into the saucers. Mike raised a smile. "You're a clumsy so-and-so. I could probably do better myself." It was a feeble joke but Tom recognized it as an attempt to be more like his usual self. Mike took two bottles out of his jacket pocket and shook a capsule out of one of them. "Antibiotics," he said tersely. The other he turned over in his hand once or twice before putting it away unopened.

"Did you see Cressida before you left?" Tom inquired. A shuttered look came into his friend's face at the mention of her name. "What did you tell her? I must know, you know. I'm bound to see her while you're away and we've got to tell the same story . . ."

"Yes . . . yes, I understand that. I just said I was going away on business — indefinitely."

"And she bought it, I suppose, with you looking like death warmed up?"

"She hadn't much time to notice . . . we said our goodbyes very quickly."

"You make it sound as though the two of you are finished." Tom's tone was puzzled.

"Tom, you can't 'finish' something

that never really began." He paused. "Oh, I admit there was a time . . . " his voice trailed away. Then he made a visible effort to pull himself together. "Cressida is a very kind girl, especially to those she considers less fortunate than herself, it is part of her training as well as her nature and I'm sure she always means it for the best. One day she may find out that it is sometimes cruel to be too kind!" The bitterness was almost tangible.

Tom felt bereft of words. The relationship between Mike and Cressida had clearly plummeted to zero. He felt angry with his fiancée's sister. Why hadn't she seen how ill Mike looked, quite forgetting that until recently he himself had been equally at fault.

On arrival at Boroughfield, Tom went to the reception desk and discovering that Arnold Ward was some distance away he returned pushing a wheelchair. They had quite an argument about it which Tom finally won. The bed was located in the side-ward. Tom hung about, uncomfortably aware that there was nothing more he could do but loth to leave Mike to face whatever was in store — alone.

"You've got a long drive back, Tom, so please go now. I'll put your name down as next-of-kin so they'll tell you what happens . . . and Tom . . . thanks for everything." The arrival of a nurse cut short further farewells then Mike was submitted to the admission formalities. Already he felt swallowed up by hospital routine.

It was not long before a doctor appeared, announcing, "I'm Abelson, Mr Ponting's registrar. You have some X-rays for me?" Mike pointed to the envelope on the locker. The doctor took them out, put them on the viewing-screen and drew in his breath sharply, he read the admission notes, and finally he examined Mike's leg, his touch gentle. When he had finished he said. "It's pretty painful, isn't it?" Mike nodded. "Mr Ponting isn't here till Monday but he wants you to have complete bed-rest, meanwhile we can get on with some tests."

Mike woke very early in the morning feeling as though he had the worst hangover of his life. The fact that he had slept at all was largely due to the sleeping-tablets they had insisted he take. Gradually it dawned on him that not all the clattering was going on inside his head, beyond the partially closed curtain he could see a pink-overalled lady laying out cups on a trolley. "Hey you!" he called.

The woman gave a start and turned round. "Oh dear! I am sorry — I didn't know there was anyone here, this room 'asn't been used for ages. I'm that sorry, sir." She pushed the trolley towards the door.

"Just a minute," Mike detained her. "Since you woke me up, how about a quick cup of tea?"

"I don't see why not since I don't start proper for half an hour." She left, returning a few minutes later with a steaming cup, which she set down on the locker.

"You must have to come in very early," commented Mike, "it's only half past five now."

"You don't know *how* early, dear; I got to come in all the way from Dunster."

Mike wondered if he'd heard right. Surely that was the name of the place where Julia and Cressida lived? But it was quite possible that there was more than one village in England with that name.

"Dunster?" He queried. "Is that far then?"

"You not from these parts?" he shook his head. "It must be all of twelve miles."

"Is there a church there, St Michael's I think it's called?" He took a sip of the tea which was excellent.

"That's right, dear."

"The vicar isn't called Maitland by any chance?"

"Yes I believe he is, someone told me

his daughter's an actress. I ain't seen her on the telly though." She picked up his empty cup. "You won't let on about this will you . . . " Mike shook his head . . . "and I'm sorry I woke you — an' you looking as if you could do with the sleep an' all." She departed leaving him with a lot to think about. No matter where he went it seemed the Fates were determined to keep him in some way linked with Cressida. Perhaps she was even now spending the weekend at the vicarage and only a few miles away.

Doctor Abelson paid another visit, flicked through the notes and rubbed a reflective hand over his chin. "Not feeling so good then?"

"I've felt better."

"I think we should consider asking Mr Ponting to come in and see you, today, if possible. I'll give him a call." Mike dozed off but the sound of voices outside his room brought him back to full awareness; Abelson had left the door open a little and he could hear two nurses chatting.

"What's the new patient in the side-ward like?"

"Youngish, good-looking . . . rather dishy in fact . . . " Mike smiled to himself.

"Is it serious? I mean he's not a private patient or anything . . . to be put in the side-ward."

"I think it must be; Abelson's phoned for old Ponting to come in on a Saturday and I heard him saying to Sister that he's almost certain to lose the leg and even that being a bit dicey in his present condition."

"God, that's awful, poor man . . . " The voices died away as their owners retreated along the corridor.

Mike was angry . . . very angry. Now that the spectre he feared most was almost upon him he wanted to get away . . . to go somewhere where he could think things out. His clothes, crutches and the caliper were still in the room. Gingerly he swung first one leg and then the other over the side of the bed. The sudden increase in pain almost gave him second thoughts but pain was something he had learned to cope with. He finished dressing and then wrote a short note and left it on his locker. He edged towards the door, still without any clear idea of what he was going to do.

A sudden torrent of sound broke out in the corridor . . . the cardiac arrest bell was ringing. There were raised voices, running footsteps, clattering trollies, there would never be a better moment to make his escape. He waited by the lift until the bell stopped ringing, not even the thought of detection would make him break the rule that the lift must not be used during an emergency. The noise ceased, he pressed the button, the doors swished open and within seconds he was on the ground floor and heading towards the main entrance.

A minicab had just pulled up and was disgorging a passenger. Suddenly he knew without question what he was going to do. He went up to the driver.

"Are you booked with another fare?" he inquired.

"No, I'm on my way back to the depot for my lunch-break, but if it's not too far . . . where d'yer wanna go, guv?"

"A village called Dunster."

"Bloody hell, that's miles away. Sorry, guv, no can do." He started to put the car in gear.

"I'll pay you extra, it's very important." Glancing anxiously back at the main door, Mike took a fifty-pound note out of his wallet. "Would that be enough to drive me there and wait for about half an hour then bring me back?"

The lure of the extra money and the look on the face of the man on crutches decided it. "OK then guv," he gave in.

Mike was too absorbed in his own thoughts to appreciate the countryside that lay round Cressida's home. Now he knew exactly where he wanted to go. In one of her confiding moments she had told him about her visits to the church when she was troubled. "There's someone there who I feel always listens to me." Although she hadn't specified who, perhaps her 'someone' would help him too.

"This is Dunster, sir; whereabouts do you want to go?"

"As close to the church as possible." The car drew up at the lychgate; there was quite a long path winding between gravestones up to the porch. "Perhaps you would be kind enough to see if the door is open?" The driver came back answering in the affirmative and helped Mike out of the car. "Come back in about half an hour; perhaps there's somewhere you can get a bite to eat since I've taken up your lunch-hour."

Even the short walk to the church door was an almost impossible exertion but as soon as he entered the cool quietness of the interior Mike knew instinctively that he had come to the right place. He sat down in one of the pews and rested his leg along its length, propping his back against the corner, letting the peace of Cressida's place enfold him, he felt deeply that her belief in its meaning was helping him to accept the future.

Arthur Maitland had inadvertently left his copy of the parish accounts in the vestry. He crossed the short distance between the vicarage and the church, feeling rather sorry that paperwork was going to keep him indoors on such a beautiful afternoon.

He unlocked the vestry door and saw the missing folder lying on one of the chairs. He was about to leave, when he suddenly decided to spend a few quiet moments in the church. He genuflected as he passed the altar on the way to his own seat at the end of the choir-stalls and as he turned to enter it he felt a spurt of anger. A man seemed to be sprawled in one of the pews — asleep — drunk perhaps.

The nave of the church was darkened as the sun plunged behind a cloud, and the Vicar's anger subsided; whatever the reason, the sleeper had been guided towards the church, it was not for him to judge but rather to extend a hand in friendship. The sun emerged again and a shaft of light struck down through a clerestory window, illuminating the head of the reclining figure. Something Cressida had once said in one of her letters came into his mind . . . 'and he has the same bronze-gold hair as St Michael of the east window'. Then with a shock he saw the crutches — what he had thought was a drunken sprawl was a man supporting an injured leg. "God forgive me," he petitioned silently. The man seemed oblivious of his presence so he was able to study him carefully; the more he looked the more certain he became that this was the Michael Carteret that Cressida had written about, and yet she had never even hinted at any form of disability. The well-worn crutches and the look of suffering, even in repose, suggested that the condition was not a temporary one.

Mike opened his eyes to find he was

no longer alone. It was not difficult to deduce that the other man must be Cressida's father. He didn't feel up to explanations and then amazingly, they weren't needed.

"Forgive me if I'm wrong but aren't you Michael Carteret?"

There was a puzzled silence before Mike replied. "No, you are quite right, but how did you know?"

Arthur smiled. "Cressida writes very good letters!"

"Oh . . . I see . . . I suppose you're wondering what I'm doing here?"

"Why you are in the church is a matter for you, but I would like to know if my daughter is here too."

With a mixture of relief and disappointment Mike realized that Cressida had not come home for the weekend after all. "No, I'm afraid she's not. I'd better come clean. I'm an escapee from Boroughfield Hospital. I had some problems I wanted to sort out and this place came highly recommended."

The vicar gave Mike a shrewd look.

"I must say your truancy doesn't look as if it's doing you any good, physically that is. Do you want to talk about it?"

"As you no doubt know I have a certain difficulty in getting about . . ." Mike gestured towards the crutches, and Arthur nodded, this was not the time to say that it had come as a complete surprise, " . . . and there is a distinct possibility that things might get worse — much worse . . . "

"Cressida knows about this?"

"No!" Mike's voice was vehement. "Absolutely not, she thinks I've gone away on business. She mustn't know . . . "

"Why not? You are friends, aren't you? She gave me that impression anyway." In fact the letters had, without actually saying so, implied a great deal more.

Mike sought around for a way of expressing what he believed his relationship with Cressida had been. "More like ships that passed, although not necessarily in the night!" he gave a wry smile. "Now we are both set on different courses."

Privately the vicar thought that the whole thing was much more complex and the discovery that Mike was disabled was an added dimension. He decided on a direct but simple approach. "Is there any way I can help?"

"I suppose a prayer or two couldn't do any harm and that's certainly more in your province than mine."

"If that was what you wanted, Boroughfield has a very nice chapel . . . much handier and under the circumstances probably less painful too!"

"As I said, this place came with very good references and Cressida was right, it is very beautiful."

The vicar tried a little drawing-out tactic. "Would it be as attractive without the personal associations?"

"That's a leading question but I won't deny that there is comfort in the thought that someone I . . . " he paused, "know and like has been here so often, but please don't tell Cressida that I came here . . . On your word of honour," his voice implored and his expression was equally anxious.

"On my word as a priest, if that is what you want." He saw Mike's features relax but sighed inwardly. A 'Road Closed' sign had been put up.

"My taxi will be back soon, I must be going, but I'm glad we met." Mike pulled himself upright and fitted the crutches. The vicar went on in front to open the heavy oak doors — and then behind him he heard a terrible sound — part groan, part cry, but all pain.

In his younger days Arthur Maitland had been a rugby player of some talent but this was to be the fastest turn and the most important catch he ever made, for Michael Carteret had collapsed — fortunately the crutches held him up for just that split second that the vicar needed, but he only just managed to prevent the unconscious figure from hitting the floor with full force, the weight taking him down too. At first he half lay, half sat there, winded, and then he took stock of the situation. Mike's left leg was doubled up underneath him, the right lay straight out in front, a dark stain spreading slowly on the trouser-leg below the knee. The vicar eased himself gently away from the younger man and retrieved a kneeler from the nearest pew, carefully resting Mike's head on it. As he did so the eyes fluttered open, then focused. "I'm sorry," the voice was barely audible, "I think my leg has broken," then he lapsed into unconsciousness again.

Mike urgently needed help but the last thing Arthur wanted to do was to leave him unattended. He went outside but not a soul could be seen. Then Mike's taxi arrived. Arthur wasted no time. "Listen," he said to the driver, "the man you brought here has been taken very ill — he needs urgent attention but I don't want to leave him. Do you see that house over there, the one with green shutters? A Doctor Wantage lives there — ask him to come to the church and bring his medical bag — and hurry."

It took about ten minutes for the doctor to arrive; immediately he was on his knees beside Mike. "What on earth's happened here?" He was already slitting Mike's trouser leg to reveal the site of the injury. "Good grief!" he exclaimed. "I'm not qualified to deal with this, he must go to hospital at once — part of the tibia has shattered and pieces of the bone are protruding . . . it's a terrible mess."

"He told me he's a patient at Boroughfield . . . "

"And that's where he ought to be as soon as possible." As he spoke the doctor was feeling carefully down the other leg. "This one seems to be all right but we'll have to straighten it out. Thank goodness the injured one is supported by this caliper, that will make our job a bit easier and help to limit the damage." The three of them working together in the cramped space achieved the task, but not without causing the semi-conscious Mike great pain.

"Now we've got the problem of getting him to hospital. I think we should use my Dormobile, it'll be quicker than calling an ambulance. But he'll still have to be got out of here somehow."

"I believe there's an old stretcher up at the vicarage." The doctor told Arthur to fetch it, together with a clean sheet and some blankets, and at the same time despatched the taxi-driver to bring the Dormobile up to the church — he gave Mike a shot of pain-killer before the move was accomplished, nevertheless the Vicar was only too aware that, during the journey, every bump and bend in the road was an agony for him. Towards the end a sort of delirium set in and Mike began to talk incoherently; he spoke Cressida's name over and over again. Her father came to believe that she must mean a great deal more to him than he had admitted.

8

SISTER ARNOLD was quivering although outwardly remaining calm; the disappearance of a patient was a very serious matter, and the moment of truth was about to arrive, she could hear his short, distinctive footfall approaching. The door was flung open and Mr Ponting announced, "I am given to understand you have re-interpreted the meaning of bed-rest, Sister! The bed is resting comfortably but what have you done with the patient?" Sister pursed her lips as he went on, "Even during a cardiac emergency I fail to see how a man on crutches — with a caliper and . . . " he consulted his clip-board " . . . and a temperature of over 101 degrees, could not only manage to leave the ward and the floor but also, it seems, the building! His progress can hardly have been that of an Olympic runner and yet none of your staff were fast enough to catch him."

"Of course I take full responsibility for what has happened Mr Ponting, it was just unfortunate that the cardiac arrest meant that his absence wasn't discovered earlier. He left this for you, she pushed Mike's note across the desk. The surgeon ripped it open and read, "I just need to be AWOL for a few hours; the idea of losing my leg, however inefficient, needs some getting used to, preferably away from this medical hothouse. Don't blame anybody for my temporary absence." It was signed 'M. Carteret'.

Mr Ponting threw the note down again. "Read that, Sister, and you will find out why your patient did a bunk. I should like to know how he was informed of my decisions before I have even made them!"

"Doctor Abelson told me he thought that would be your recommendation, once you had seen the X-rays. But we were alone in the office at the time. I can only suppose that someone overheard and discussed the matter within Mr Carteret's hearing."

"Well in future I hope you will instruct your nurses that what they 'overhear' must not be transmitted . . . under any circumstances; you can see what it can lead to." Before she could reply the surgeon's bleeper sounded. He picked up the phone. "Ponting." He listened and then said. "At once, I'm on my way. That is your errant patient, Sister — returned to our tender care. It seems that he now has a very messy spontaneous fracture of the right tibia and massive complications." His parting shot as he left the office was . . . "Oh, and if by any chance he comes back onto this ward — he will probably be unconscious, perhaps you will be able to keep him in his bed then!"

Ponting swept the curtain of the casualty cubicle aside. He barked out demands for vital signs, gently lifted the sterile cloth covering Mike's leg and without pausing for breath ordered a theatre and all its equipment to be readied immediately. "If I can save this leg it will be largely thanks to the people who got him here and who kept their heads." He then gave his attention to Mike's general condition. "The leg is one thing, his life is another, that may need a miracle. Now I must have a word with the two who brought him in."

Doctor Wantage and the vicar were waiting in the reception area. Mr Ponting bore down on them, and spoke to the younger man first. "You did a damned good job, there's reason to hope that I can save that leg now . . . Silly young fool, leaving the hospital like that! I want to know if he's eaten anything or if you gave any medication." Arthur shook his head and Wantage named the painkiller. "He keeps calling out a name . . . Cassandra . . . something like that. Can either of you tell me who she might be?"

"Yes, she's my daughter, Cressida."

"Wife? . . . Fiancée?"

"No, neither. I think he . . . "

The surgeon cut him short. "Could you get her here?"

"I could try. Why, what good would it do?"

"That's more your department, vicar. My skill and modern science and technology, can only do so much. In a case like this the will to live is all-important. There's not much good my fighting to save his leg if he doesn't fight to save his own life. If he wants her then she should be here."

A nurse approached. "I'm afraid the intensive care unit is full, Mr Ponting — but everything you want will be put into the side-ward on Arnold."

"Hmph, that will please Sister, I don't think!" He turned to Arthur . . . "What about relatives?"

"I'm afraid I don't know, but I can find out."

"Do that then. I must go now, the theatre will be ready." He marched off.

Arthur addressed Doctor Wantage. "I can't thank you enough for coming to my assistance so promptly — it seems that we, or rather you, did all the right things. Now I don't want you to wait for me . . . "

"Well. If you're sure," the doctor sounded doubtful, "but you will keep me posted, won't you?" The two men shook hands. Arthur knew it was going to be difficult to tell Cressida that she was needed and at the same time keep his vow to Mike. If she asked questions he would just have to bend the truth a little.

He was allowed to use the chaplain's office to phone from, only to discover that Cressida was out, Julia didn't know where. She was very taken aback by the news that Mike was in hospital. "The thing is, Julia, I think it essential that Tom and Cressida should come up here right away. Mike is critically ill and his surgeon believes that her presence, particularly, might help to pull him through." Julia agreed at once to get in touch with Tom, and to pack a bag for her sister so they could set off as soon as she could be found.

★ ★ ★

Cressida had no idea where she was — one high-hedged lane looked much like another and she was wrestling with her problems rather than taking in the beauties of the landscape. Had Mike finally decided that the barrier of his disability was an insuperable wall between them which he was unable to scale and which he wouldn't permit her to? Or was it that he had just become bored with her? In either case there was no solution. A car screeched up beside her, the passenger door was opened and a peremptory voice said, "Get in!" It was Tom Blakeney.

"I beg your pardon." Cressida's look was withering, she was not one to be spoken to in that manner.

Tom modified his approach. "I've been driving all round the countryside looking for you — now will you please get in?" The anger died out of his expression but it remained grave and unsmiling.

"I came out for a walk, not a drive . . . "

"You're wanted . . . urgently . . . now! Get in and I'll tell you . . . please," he repeated.

Cressida gave in and climbed into the car. "What's the matter, Tom, and why so urgent?"

"Before I tell you, will you answer one question?"

"Maybe." She didn't like commitments in advance. Tom went on as though she hadn't spoken.

"What are your real feelings for Mike?"

"I don't think that's any of your business," she replied brusquely.

"I'm making it my business, and before you get on your high horse, please believe me when I say I have a very good reason for asking." He seemed so serious.

"Mike and I are or rather were . . . " she paused "good friends, but now he's made it quite clear he doesn't want to continue after he comes back from his business trip."

Tom's voice was considerably softer as he replied. "He's not away on business, he's in hospital . . . "

Cressida grabbed his arm. "Hospital! I knew he wasn't well! Is that why you were looking for me? Tell me!"

Tom couldn't repress a smile of relief. She had told him what he wanted to know. "Calm down, girl, and let go of my arm, you'll cause an accident."

"Sorry. But for God's sake tell me about it!"

"I can see that Mike means a great deal to you — much more than just friends." She nodded. "Then I'll tell you what little I know. I took Mike to Boroughfield yesterday." Cressida looked puzzled when she heard the name but said nothing. "It seems that it is not far from your father's parish and he was visiting someone there; I don't know the details, but he must have found out somehow that Mike was there and critically ill. He thinks we should be there."

Cressida was far from the silent companion that Mike had been. "I don't understand why he went to that particular hospital, it's so far from his home?"

"But not all that far from where the accident occurred, and it has the best orthopaedic unit in the Midlands. He was a patient there for over a year."

"He never talks about what happened . . . " She hoped that Tom might be prepared to, but his next remark removed that hope.

"If he hasn't told you, you can hardly expect me to, now can you?"

"He gives very little away about himself, he's so reserved and self-controlled."

"That's largely because he's afraid of being a drag. I've hoped for such a long time that he could find someone to relax and share some of his inner feelings with. He won't with me because he thinks it will just increase my guilt. He'll never tell you this, but I should have driven the car that crashed; it was a mechanical fault, not his. It was soon after Anna's death, so he went in my place . . . and was crippled as a result," his voice was harsh.

A little while later Cressida said worriedly, "I hope you're not expecting some sort of bedside romance, Tom! Whatever my feelings I'm pretty certain he doesn't feel the same about me. Oh I know he felt an attraction, but I don't believe it reached his heart at all."

"I'm not so sure . . . but now that he wants you, you'll be there and that's the main thing."

"No, Tom, the main thing is that he's still alive."

★ ★ ★

Cressida's father was able to assure them both that Mike had come through the operation but it was still very much touch and go.

"What do they want me to do? When can I see him?" asked Cressida anxiously.

At that moment Mr Ponting trotted into view. "Well, is she here?" The vicar introduced Cressida. The surgeon wasted no time on formalities. "Good, come with me — I'll explain why I wanted you as we go." Cressida gave them a last appealing look and they made a reassuring thumbs-up sign.

"Miss Maitland, I'm not interested in your private affairs with the patient so spare me the details. I've asked you to come because you seem to be on his mind and are therefore the best person to relate to him." They reached Arnold Ward and went into Sister's office. There was a plate of sandwiches and a pot of tea on the desk. "Those are for you but don't drink too much, you mightn't get many chances of leaving the room in the next hours. I must brief you on what to expect when you go in.

I have had to take part of one of his ribs to repair the damage to his leg — a severe enough procedure in any event, without all his added complications.

You will find him surrounded by all the apparatus of modern medical technology but you must ignore all that and think of him as the man you know. And now for the most important part. You will hold his hand, talk to him if he's comatose, calm him if he's delirious, in fact do everything you can to make him realize that you are there, fighting every inch of the way with him. It is your job to try and keep him in contact with this world and not let him slip through our fingers into the next. It won't be easy or quick either. Are you ready for it?"

"I'm ready, Mr Ponting, but will I be able?" Cressida's voice was full of uncertainty.

His expression softened. "If you want it enough and I think you do, you'll be able." Five minutes later she entered Mike's room.

Although she had been warned what to expect it still came as a shock, he was almost like a being from another planet. His eyes were open but their feverish brilliance held no recognition. She sat down and took hold of his hand, it was hot and dry. At first she felt shy and embarrassed to talk to someone in his condition. She began tentatively at first, then gradually she forgot the surroundings and began the long, one-sided conversation. Sometimes he lay quiet. There were times when he clung onto her so tightly that it hurt. She watched as a beard grew on increasingly hollow cheeks and she felt the bones of his hand become more prominent. Sometimes he called out . . . "I can't . . . I can't hold it . . . " and she was sure he was reliving his car crash.

The routine care of the patient flowed around her, she hardly touched the plates of things they brought for her to eat, and she snatched the briefest of respites when his grip relaxed. By the end of the second day every part of her ached and her voice was hoarse. She had encouraged him, cajoled him, coaxed him, and calmed him, but at no time did she ever speak of love or allow emotion to break through; not, that is, until nearly the end of the second night.

Sheer exhaustion had caused her head to droop forward. Suddenly he called out her name, begging her, in his delirium, 'not to go without him'. For the last thirty-six hours she had tried so hard to reassure him with her touch and her voice, now all she had left were her tears. "Oh, my darling I'll never go anywhere without you if you promise not to leave me, I need you so very much." She cradled his hand against her cheek and the tears ran down her face and over his lean fingers and then she kissed them willing her life and strength to flow into him. Time passed, her mind clouded with tiredness; still holding the hand against her face she rested her head on the bed and fell asleep.

Mr Ponting's hand on her shoulder brought her back to awareness and she started to apologize. "My dear, your job is over . . . look." For a moment a cold hand gripped her heart, then she raised her head and saw that Mike was sleeping peacefully at last. "He's out of danger now. Of course his leg is going to take a long time to heal, months rather than weeks, but I'm hopeful of a good result there too — certainly the pain he's suffered recently will be gone.

"Your father's waiting for you. I order twenty-four hours in bed before you come back and see Michael."

"I won't be coming back. I don't even want him to know I was here. Please don't tell him."

"That will be a very difficult request to fulfil, young lady, hospitals being what they are. So many people know you were here. Someone's almost bound to talk." The surgeon was puzzled. "Why don't you want him to know, you did as much as any of us to save his life."

"That's just it. I don't want to oblige him to feel grateful . . . or . . . " Cressida hunted in her tired mind for the words to express her feelings " . . . or to seem to have been taken advantage of in some way . . . and so add to all the other things he has to contend with."

"Ah! Now I do understand. I will do what I can. He may know anyway, when he wakes up."

Cressida thought for a moment. "I think the chances are that he won't; he gave no sign that he recognized me."

If she had been less tired, less distraught, in those moments before Mike fell into a true sleep she might have heard the thinnest thread of sound coming from his lips: "Cressy — is that you?" But she had not.

"Oh Dad! Mike's going to get better. Isn't that wonderful?" Cressida threw her arms round her father, then she frowned. "What day is it? I'm confused."

"It's Monday; you've been here since Saturday evening."

Suddenly she remembered. "What about the Foundation? Half-term is over — I haven't told them."

"Relax, Cressy, Tom has taken care of everything. Julia has got herself a really good man at last." It had always been the vicar's worry that his beautiful elder daughter, who attracted men without the slightest effort, might so easily choose the wrong one.

Cressida felt incredibly lively and wide-awake, but Arthur recognized the symptoms of delayed reaction, she needed to unwind before she would get any real rest. He urged her to go to bed and he would bring her up some of Mrs P's chicken soup. He carried the tray up to her room and found her standing staring out of the window. "Mike's going to be all right, you know . . . "

"And Mr Ponting was able to save his leg and I'm so happy for him . . . and I love him so much, Daddy, and he doesn't want me — except when he's delirious . . . " She burst into an uncontrollable storm of tears. He just stood there holding her until it had dissolved into hiccupy sobs, then helped her into the bed.

"Now you've got that out of your system — have some of Mrs Plunkett's excellent soup, and tell me all about it." Cressida smiled weakly and held the cup in both hands.

"Dad, I want you to promise me not to tell Mike when you see him, as I'm sure you will, that I was with him for all that time. I've asked Mr Ponting not to either and to see if he can prevent the staff from doing so."

The vicar had not expected this. "Whyever not?"

"I must explain to you, Dad, that whatever Mike might say in delirium, in his conscious mind he doesn't even want me as a friend any more. He didn't even tell me he was going into hospital, but I love him, Dad and even if there's only the faintest glimmer of hope that he may change his mind I don't want him to think that he has an obligation to me. Does that make sense?"

"I suppose it does." Arthur saw another 'Road Closed' sign go up. "I promise," he said, and gave a little sigh.

She handed him the empty soup-cup and snuggled down into the bed. "Where's Tom, has he gone back to Seahaven?"

"Oh, I forgot to tell you, he got in touch with Mike's mother; it was very lucky, she was in New York for a few days, so she flew over at once. Tom's gone to the airport to meet her, they should be at the hospital by now."

"I'm so glad, he'll be pleased to see his mother." Cressida's voice was beginning to sound drowsy. Arthur drew the curtains across, then slipped quietly out.

★ ★ ★

At about the same time that Cressida fell asleep, Mike woke up. He lay with his eyes closed trying to gather the fragments of memory together. The last clear image he had was of being in a church . . . Cressida's church; he was talking to her father. Beyond that nothing seemed to fit properly; then out of the haze a picture emerged; he was sure Cressida had been with him; he could feel the sensation of his hand in hers and something wet against the back of it. He opened his eyes. A woman with a halo of blonde hair was sitting by the bed. For a moment he couldn't focus properly and then he heard a familiar voice say his name.

"Mother? . . . Didn't know you were here." His lips and throat were dry and the words difficult to form.

"I came as soon as I heard, on the very first flight." She leaned forward and kissed him on the forehead. He began to drift off to sleep again — it was marvellous of his mother to come all this way, but somehow the thought was tinged with disappointment — it must have been her he saw earlier ... and yet ... and yet ... why had he sensed Cressida's presence so strongly?

9

TOM came back two days later to collect Cressida. He paid a quick visit to the hospital first. She could hardly wait to hear the latest news. "He still feels pretty ropy — not up to talking much yet, but they seem pleased with his progress and his mother was there."

On the journey they discussed what they should or shouldn't say to Mike. She was adamant that he should not discover that she had been at his bedside . . . "I'm not even supposed to know that he's ill! You were not allowed to tell me, remember?" In the end they decided that it was only natural that Tom would have told her that Mike had been very ill. "Right then, if he asks, just say you had to tell me, but not when! Will you be going back to Boroughfield soon?"

"Probably the weekend after next — Julia too."

"Then I'll come as well, and it won't look like a special visit — from me, I mean."

* * *

During the next ten days Cressida found herself inhabiting a strange half-world. Physically she had recovered from the ordeal and went back to work on the Thursday. Everyone was glad that she had recovered from her bout of 'flu'. Her mind, however, felt as though it was fighting through cotton wool. All her thoughts seemed fuzzy and unreal — even the hours spent at Mike's bedside began to feel as if they had happened to someone else. She did make one decision and that was to write a brief note to Mike. She wanted to prepare him for the visit she intended making.

Although Tom had come with her to the hospital, Cressida went in to see

Mike alone. His leg was still supported in its strange-looking cradle but all the other paraphernalia had gone. His now clean-shaven face had lost the drawn mask-like quality it had had when she last saw him but there was still evidence of his desperate fight for life.

The visit was not a success; not that Cressida had really expected it to be. The theory of concealment was one thing, the practice of it quite another; it was against her very nature. She found herself restlessly fiddling with things and making superficial small talk which was punctuated by awkward silences.

She had hoped, perhaps too optimistically, that the attitude he had taken in 'The Smugglers' on the night before he had gone on his so-called 'business trip' would have softened, but it appeared not to have done.

Cressida wanted desperately to put her arms around him and just hold him, so that she could be thankful for the gift of his life. There were so many words of love she wanted to say, so many she wanted to hear. Instead they seemed to have nothing important to say to each other; finally she observed, "You look tired, Mike, I think I'd better go."

"Yes, you've done your good deed for the day. I'm quite surprised you didn't bring grapes. They're the traditional gift from those visiting the sick, aren't they?" He knew he was being unnecessarily unkind. His hand clenched and unclenched beneath the bedclothes. Oh God, why did she have to come and tighten the clamps on his heart. But of course she was doing no such thing; she was, in her kind, generous way, giving her time to a friend in hospital, no more, no less. He took refuge in invalidism to apologize. "I'm sorry, that was very rude, please forget I said it; but you're right I am a bit tired today. I'm not very good company." He didn't ask her to come again.

Her face showed the hurt he had inflicted and he felt ashamed, especially when she tried to hide it by saying with a little smile, "I didn't bring you grapes but I brought you this instead." She laid a tissue-wrapped package on the locker. He put his hand out to take it. "No," she stopped him, "don't open it till I've gone. Oh yes, and I nearly forgot, my father wants to know if you would like him to come and see you?"

"Please tell him, yes, whenever he likes . . . and thank you for coming," he added, "it was kind of you." She sketched a little wave and was gone.

For a long time he looked at the little parcel without opening it. At last he took it off the locker and unwrapped the layers of tissue paper. Finally it lay revealed, a polished wooden plaque, only a few inches square, but exquisitely carved in relief on its shiny, chestnut-coloured surface was a horse's head, on which had been carefully hand-painted a white star, making it a perfect likeness of Horace. The thought of the care Cressida had taken in the choice of such a gift made him grip it so hard, the knuckles stood out white. "Damn, damn, damn . . . " he exclaimed under his breath.

* * *

In the weeks that followed the Reverend Arthur Maitland became one of Mike's regular visitors. Leaving the hospital after a visit, Mr Ponting caught up with him. "Could you spare me a few moments?"

"Of course, what can I do for you?"

"It isn't so much what you can do for me, rather for Michael Carteret. I have been discussing his case with the cardio-vascular consultant here, and, using new techniques, he believes that he can restore the left leg to at least eighty per cent normality. It should be quite all right to go ahead with it fairly soon."

"That sounds marvellous. What's the problem?"

"Mike won't listen. He only has to

hear the word 'operation' and he just switches off."

"How many has he had already?"

"Only one major one this time and a couple of examinations and replasterings under general anaesthetic. I'd have to look up the records for the others — fourteen or fifteen, I should think."

"Isn't that your answer, he just doesn't want another?"

"Possibly, but I think there's more to it than that. Oh, he's still very co-operative, does his exercises, takes his medications, doesn't complain, but the enthusiasm for recovery that was there before is somehow missing . . . it's not easy to put one's finger on."

"You had better tell me a bit more about the first time."

"Both his legs were severely damaged, the right had multiple fractures, including the ankle and the hip, particularly bad was the lower leg with a great deal of fragmentation. I thought I would lose it but I managed to put most of it back together, of course it ended up shorter and with a considerable loss of function. The recent problem was due to an infection causing some of the ironmongery that I had to put in coming adrift. Am I making myself clear?"

The vicar assented . . . "But from what you say it seems he will always be very lame; if another operation won't alter that perhaps he doesn't think it's worth it."

"It is, to this extent. If he has this operation I believe he might eventually be able to walk with a stick and give up crutches altogether. The agonizing muscle cramps he suffers would be gone. Be a good chap and see if you can make him change his mind."

At his next visit Arthur came straight out with the question: "Why won't you have the operation Mr Ponting recommends?"

"It won't be a miracle cure you know. I'll still be a cripple even if it works." His voice held an unaccustomed bitterness.

"What makes you think it won't?"

"Good God! Do you think I haven't been through it all before, and I still ended up . . . well you know that bit. Why should I believe them now?"

"Not having to use crutches is surely a big improvement? Worth just one more operation."

"Perhaps, but I'm not sure that I care anymore."

"Other people might." Before he could stop himself the vicar went on, "Cressida might. Tom might. Your mother might. Don't you think all the people who have been rooting for you to get well would be pleased? Are you going to let them down by not trying this one last time?" Was he being unfair? He turned away, not wanting to see the result of his outburst.

The reply was unexpected. "I can see where Cressida gets her directness from, but I suppose you're right, I should let them try . . . this one last time," he echoed the vicar's words.

Then a note of humour crept into his voice: "Anyway it would be nice to do without those damn crutches; wherever one puts them, they always fall down!"

After Arthur left, Mike picked up the little carving that Cressida had given him, his fingers caressing the smooth, polished wood. If only it were a miracle cure, he thought, then he would gladly do anything that would earn him the right to . . . at that point he put a full stop to wishful thinking.

The operation took place the following week and was an unqualified success.

* * *

Five months had passed since Mike had been admitted. Mr Ponting would have liked him to be able to leave hospital, but he didn't want him too far away because the leg still needed frequent attention and physiotherapy.

Once again he addressed the problem to the vicar who immediately suggested a ground-floor room at the vicarage. "When will he be able to come?"

"Shall we say the beginning of next week?"

Mike left the hospital with strict instructions not to overdo things and to go back every week for treatment.

★ ★ ★

For Cressida the weeks were sliding drearily one into another. In her mind she often went over the brief time she and Mike had spent together. The painting of the Pasque Flower he had given her had pride of place in her room and she often lay on the bed staring hopelessly at it. Every avenue seemed to be closed to her, and the news that he was living at the vicarage meant that a visit there was now impossible too.

Julia got thoroughly fed up with living with what she called an emotional zombie. "Look here, Cressy, no man is worth all this angst; forget him or go and tell him."

"But you don't understand, Julia, I have been to see him and he doesn't want me to go again."

"You should be pleased about that."

"What on earth do you mean?" Cressida exclaimed.

"Just this, sister dear — when we last had this discussion you said, 'If he really loves me and won't say so because he's disabled, he wouldn't even want me near him!'" Julia quoted triumphantly. "Anyway I can't think why this is such a problem when everyone says you're so good at sorting them out."

"What sort of 'everyone'?"

"Oh I don't know . . . complete strangers to me . . . down here they're always talking about the wonderful things you're doing at the Foundation. I recall one occasion very clearly . . . in 'The Smugglers'. I was waiting for Tom — it was the day we'd been on that shopping trip . . . and it was raining — you remember."

"It's not an evening I'm likely to

forget," said Cressida dully. "Go on then, Ju, what happened?"

"I suppose the laugh was on me really. This woman came up to me and said, 'I hope you don't mind but aren't you Julia Maitland?' I thought she wanted an autograph but it was you she wanted to talk about . . . the Foundation and so on."

"And what did you say to that?"

"I don't remember exactly . . . something about how you were always so good with children and lame dogs . . . "

"You said what!" Cressida exploded. "When? I mean what time was it when you said it?"

"Let me think — Tom and I were going on to a film in Seahaven . . . I suppose it must have been sometime between seven and half past . . . "

"Oh my God! Don't you see, Julia . . . Mike was there, waiting for me, he must have overheard you . . . he must have thought . . . Good God, what *must* he have thought! How could you have said such a dreadful thing?"

"I didn't know Mike was there." Julia's voice was defensive.

"It was a damned insensitive remark to make at any time," Cressida retorted angrily. "Not much wonder he didn't want anything more to do with me after that. He must have thought he was just an extension of my social work . . . or a charity case to be patronized — and just when he needed to trust me most."

"I'm sorry, Cress, I didn't mean anything like that . . . "

"That's all very well, but what on earth can I do about it? He'll never believe anything I say now — so much for your damned theories, Julia!"

For once Julia accepted that the best thing she could offer was silence.

★ ★ ★

Arthur was finding it particularly enjoyable having someone else living at the vicarage again. Despite the age difference they shared views and interests in common with enough variation to make their conversations lively affairs, but Mike never invited any discussion about Cressida and yet the vicar knew that for both their sakes the subject ought to be tackled.

The opportunity came one evening when his paperwork was interrupted by a phone call from her. She was delighted to find out how well Mike was progressing and that the two of them got on so well together, but there was no mistaking the pain in her voice and her anguished refusal to come home and see for herself. The vicar made up his mind, abandoned his letters and crossed the hall to knock on Mike's door.

"Come in." Mike was bent over the table deeply absorbed in his painting. Without looking up he said, "Sit yourself down, I won't be a minute." He completed what he was doing with a few deft strokes of the brush and then washed it vigorously in the water-pot and dried it carefully on some blotting-paper. "Sorry about that, but wash has to be applied quickly or it goes all wrong."

"I came in to say that Cressy just phoned . . . she wanted to know how you were."

Mike's smile faded, "I hope you told her I was fine."

"Yes I did. I could have added that I thought you work too hard, now that Tom has brought your computer terminal up here, and what with that, and the Christmas cards you're doing for the church roof fund . . . "

"I hope you didn't, it might give her something else to be . . . to be . . . kind to me about."

"Is that what you think?"

"I have good reason to," he answered shortly.

"Really? Don't you think it might be a good idea if we talked about it?"

"Perhaps." Mike smiled a little tiredly. "Since you're her father and my host I probably owe you an explanation of some sort." He got up from the desk and went over to a cupboard. "Would you like a beer before I start?" Arthur nodded. He took two cans out. "Catch!" He threw one over to the vicar and putting the other in his pocket he crossed the room to the other armchair and eased himself in, leaning the crutches against the wall. The silence was broken by the 'fsst! fsst!' of two can-rings being pulled. At last Mike began.

"I don't know if anyone told you what happened when we first met? How Julia and Tom and I deliberately concealed from Cressida the fact that I was crippled . . . " He saw the expression on the vicar's face and went on quickly. "It wasn't meant to hurt her, or last for more than one evening, but then I wasn't meant to . . . " Mike paused, searching for the right words . . . "to become so involved but I did — and I thought she began to feel something too, but above all she thought . . . " his voice dropped . . . "she believed I was a whole man."

"Go on." For Arthur, things were starting to make sense.

"I'm afraid you will think I behaved very stupidly but I persuaded the other two to help me carry on the charade for a bit longer, and one way and another it was kept up for several weeks . . . You're sure she never told you all this?" Mike gave his companion a penetrating look but the vicar's dissenting reply seemed perfectly sincere. "Well you can see the whole thing was bound to fall apart and eventually it did. Cressida must have told you how that happened at least!"

"Not a word. In fact she never told me you were lame even. It was only when we met in the church that day, that I found out . . . "

Mike sat upright. "In that case how did you know it was me? I remember you came and asked if my name was Michael Carteret. I was sure it was because you had put two and two together when you saw the crutches."

The vicar shook his head. "I believe I told you then that Cressida writes good letters; she said a great deal about you, she mentioned the sailing, how much she liked being with you . . . things like that . . . and often too."

"They would hardly help to identify a complete stranger by sight though, would they?"

"No, true enough, but there was another factor." He then went on to tell Mike about Cressida and the east window . . . "And who knows, perhaps it really was guidance from above. Anyway, that is how I guessed who you were, it had nothing to do with you being disabled. If it wasn't even worth a mention in a letter it can hardly matter to Cressida very much, can it?"

Mike digested this piece of information in silence. A silence suddenly broken by the sound of a beer-can being crushed . . . "Or I don't matter to her very much . . . "

Arthur's mind went back to the hours she had spent at Mike's bedside, using her love to strengthen his will to live, all of which he was debarred from revealing because of the promise he had given. He'd better try another approach. "You can't have it both ways, you know?"

"What do you mean?"

"For all her outgoing nature, Cressida doesn't wear her heart on her sleeve any more, it has been damaged too often for that, mostly by men who only used her as a way of getting to know Julia. I used to watch, helpless, as with varying degrees of subtlety they gained entrée into the family through her and then turned their attentions to her sister. It made her very wary of any man who seemed to take an interest in her. I probably didn't handle the situation very well either — my wife would have been so much better at it," he sighed.

"I didn't know . . . "

"Cressy wouldn't be likely to tell

you, but I can tell you this, if you have any reason to believe that she responded to you in more than a friendly way then you can be sure her true feelings were involved."

The shameful memory of the only real kiss he had given her and the brutal way he had ended it, killing her warm, loving response, came flooding back. He looked away and the vicar could see his jaw tighten.

"I can see from your face that you have in fact had such an experience; I won't ask what it was but I beg you to consider it in the light of what I have told you." Arthur felt that at last he was beginning to make some impression on the younger man's iron reserve.

"But it was before she knew about these," he gestured towards the crutches.

The Vicar allowed himself a silent shout of triumph; Mike had played into his hands, exactly as he had hoped.

"And of course then — once you had told her you couldn't walk without them, her whole attitude changed? Instantly you became an object of pity? No longer — how did you put it, 'a whole man'. Your company became her duty, not her pleasure . . . you felt embarrassed by her over-assiduous attentions . . . a mere charity case . . . "

"Stop, Arthur, for goodness sake!" Mike raised his voice to drown out the vicar's accusations and then dropped it to an emotion-filled whisper. "It never made the slightest difference, it really didn't seem to matter to her."

It was time to leave Mike to think things over for himself. "I'm going to make us some coffee."

If the vicar had helped to solve one of Mike's problems, the other had been doubled. As the months had gone by he had discovered, rather to his surprise, that far from diminishing, his love for Cressida had grown stronger, even though he believed that a corresponding response from her was only a hopeless dream. Now that Arthur had convinced him that her feelings, too, might be involved, he saw that as an even more hopeless situation.

Before his accident he had had a 'choosey but uncommitted' attitude to girlfriends. Occasionally he had believed himself in love, which had resulted in torrid but short-lived relationships. But real love? God, he hadn't the slightest idea of the meaning of it till he met Cressida. Oh yes, it meant wanting her physically, so much so that his whole being ached with desire for her, but he knew now that it also meant much, much more — it meant doing what was best for her, caring for her needs first, and that meant never shackling her to his disability or imprisoning her within his limitations. The little spark of hope that the vicar had kindled was smothered before it could catch fire.

The door opened and Arthur backed in, carrying a tray. When he turned round and saw the look in Mike's dark eyes and the camouflaging smile summoned up from some uncharted depths, he could see that his victory of a few minutes ago had only been that of a battle. The war was still to be won.

★ ★ ★

Mike returned from his latest session at the hospital full of good news. Mr Ponting had indicated that the full-length plaster with its external pinning could probably be removed soon and be replaced by a walking-plaster. He wanted to share the excitement with someone but the vicar was out.

They didn't meet again till supper time and then Mike could see at once that his news would have to wait. Arthur seemed very upset. "Do you want to talk about whatever it is that's troubling you," Mike asked quietly.

"I'm sorry, Mike, I'm afraid I'm poor company this evening. I get very depressed after funerals."

"Please tell me about it." No one

knew better than Mike the loneliness of not having anyone to talk to. "I can be a good listener you know?"

"The man who died was a violinist, his wife is a pianist, together they travelled all over the world bringing music to all sorts of out-of-the way places and they were always such fun. They used to give concerts or talks in the village about their amusing or sometimes hair-raising experiences. It was a strange thing but you only had to be in their company for a little while and you forgot all about one of them being blind. His wife stood by the graveside looking completely lost and I felt so inadequate . . . so useless."

Mike exclaimed, "I can understand why you're so concerned, she must have depended on him a great deal."

Arthur gave Mike a shrewd look. "Yes she did, he was the strong one but I think you've got the wrong end of the stick, Mike. It was John who was blind, not his wife." He observed the frowning look on Mike's face. "I don't think you believe it possible for a man to be as I have described and have what some might consider to be an insuperable handicap. Am I right?"

Mike weighed his words very carefully. "I think it is very difficult for others to see it like that — they see a handicapped or disabled person and his or her wife or husband, and draw their own conclusions. The only way for such a person — for me — to be treated as an equal in the world is to be seen not to be dependent on anyone or to be a drag on them."

The Vicar exploded. "Rubbish! . . . I've had a great deal of respect for your opinions, Mike, but now you're talking absolute nonsense and what's more I think you know it! If two people love each other they can take anything 'the world', as you call it, can throw at them. I wasn't talking about equality or independence or false pride. I'm talking about love, Mike, real love. Do you think I value the sort of 'independence' I've had since my wife died — do you think that poor woman whose husband I buried is looking forward to her 'independence'? Believe me, a loving partnership is far more important." He stopped; Mike's face was turned away and he was swirling the remains of his wine round and round the glass . . . "And if I were you, I'd jolly well get my act together before it's too late! Think about it." Arthur rose from the table and left the room, praying that Mike would come to his senses at last.

Mike sat on, alone in the dining-room, staring into the middle distance, fiddling with the glass. He had to admit that much of what Arthur had said was true. The emphasis he had put on the value of independence, his and Cressida's, he could see now might be wrong, and perhaps he had been incredibly stupid to interpret Julia's remark in the way he had, but was it too late? Had he rejected Cressida once too often? He went into his room and selecting a graphics disk, switched on the computer.

10

CRESSIDA arrived at the Foundation one Monday to find her staff in a state of great excitement. They hustled her towards the large classroom. She stood in the doorway, her eyes widening in amazement. All round the room the yellow walls she disliked so much had been decorated by a frieze of brightly-coloured pictures. For a moment she couldn't think who was responsible and then she knew that somehow Mike had organized it all.

There on the walls were all the stories they had talked about: Bo-Peep, Little Boy Blue, Goldilocks and the others, and just as she had imagined it they were set in a continuous landscape of meadows and trees. The whole of the end wall was different: set in front of a mellow brick house was a silvery lake with a small sailboat on it; in a nearby paddock a chestnut horse was grazing peacefully and at the end of a short drive a pair of wrought iron gates stood open.

She felt her eyes begin to fill with tears, and made an escape to her office followed by cries of "The children will love them," and "Why didn't you tell us?" Lying on her desk was a long, silver-coloured box containing a single crimson rose — Mike's message was crystal clear.

She tried ringing the vicarage in her lunch-break but maddeningly there was no reply. The rest of the day dragged by interminably and the moment she got back to the cottage she tried again. This time her father answered. "I'm coming home at the weekend . . . and there's something I must talk to Mike about, is he there?"

Her father said, "Now don't panic, Cressida — he's in hospital . . ." Arthur heard a terrible cry of anguish from the other end. "It's all right, my dear, he's only gone in to have what he calls 'the scaffolding' taken off his leg, it has to be done under general anaesthetic."

"Oh thank God!" The relief in her voice was a tangible thing. "When will he be back?"

"Tomorrow sometime, I think, but why have you changed your mind?"

"It was Mike who changed his . . . " A thought suddenly struck her. "It wasn't because of anything you told him, was it?" she asked anxiously.

"No, my dear," her father reassured her, "your secret is safe."

"Then expect me in time for lunch on Saturday and tell him I'm coming."

The vicar put the phone down, well satisfied with his efforts so far.

Tom dropped in at the cottage that evening to find out how everything had gone at the Foundation, because of course it was he who had translated Mike's designs for the classroom into the correct-size panels. Cressida learned how they had been downlined from

Mike's computer to the one at the yard and then built and painted to his exact specification in Blakeney's workshops. She could understand all that, but she was still puzzled about how they were put into the classroom, apparently without any fuss being made. She asked how that had been managed.

"By a little gentle string-pulling, I believe. Mike didn't think you'd mind too much and even Mrs Sinclair, who came to see it while it was being put up, was impressed." She told Tom of her intended visit to Dunster. "I'm very glad, Cressy." He put his hand on her shoulder and gave it a little squeeze. "No one deserves happiness more than you."

Cressida arrived at the vicarage in plenty of time for lunch. From her father's letters she knew Mike was using the dining-room. Now that she was about to see him again her excitement turned to nervousness; after all she had no real idea what kind of reception she would get. Her knock was answered.

Just the sound of his voice after so many months thrilled her. She went swiftly towards him.

"Oh, Mike, I don't know what to say — how to thank you for such a wonderful present for the children." She wanted to kiss him, but not even the gift of the murals had given her that right. She sat beside him, placing the folder she was carrying on the floor.

"I must admit that to please you was my first objective — but it was good to be able to do something for the Foundation too. I've missed you, Cressida — very much. I've been such a fool, good friends are hard to come by."

So they were to be friends again and friendship was surely better than nothing. "Dad said you'd had to go back to have another operation; is your leg doing all right?"

"It's just fine." He caught her doubtful glance. "Really it is ... of course it will take time, but the other one is almost as good as new now, thanks to Mr Ponting and your father. I owe him an awful lot."

Cressida grinned. "I'm just so glad he thought of having you here." She picked up the folder. "Now I've brought a lot of things to show you. These are from the children at the nursery; every child has said thank you in some way, even the very youngest . . . " Cressida could tell by his silence that he was quite overcome. She pulled a letter out of the pile. "This one is from Karen, you remember, she was the little girl we bought the dress for?" It said: 'Thank you for yore nice pitures. I hop yore legs get betr soon. lov karen.'

"I hope you don't mind my telling them about you, but they do so want you to come and see them sometime, and it's much better, even with little ones to tell the truth from the start . . . "

Mike looked at her, and then said with a wry smile, "And better with grown-ups too, don't you think?"

At that moment they could both

hear the front door opening. Cressida rushed out to greet her father. The vicar hugged her, then said, I'd like you to meet Dr Wantage, I've asked him round for a spot of lunch. Go and get Mike to join us for a drink."

The doctor was Arthur's secret weapon, there were things he could reveal that the vicar himself was debarred from saying because of the vows he had given. Now he just had to trust that the disclosures that Wantage was sure to make would have the desired effect.

Over sherry the doctor seemed very interested in Cressida's work — but she only had eyes for Mike, it was as if the desert of her life could only flower in his presence. The conversation flowed around her, and her responses were becoming automatic, Mike's proximity was overwhelming. "I'm sorry, doctor, I didn't hear what you said, do you mind saying it again?" Wantage raised his voice so that everyone in the room could hear.

"I was saying that you must have been absolutely exhausted after staying awake for over thirty-six hours — not many would have been able to do what you did." He turned to Mike. "I know Mr Ponting thinks that this young lady's extraordinary vigil by your bedside was instrumental in your recovery. Isn't that so?"

Mike said nothing — he just looked across at Cressida. Doctor Wantage went on, quite unaware of the impact he was having . . . "But I do feel that the vicar and I must claim some success, what we did in the church probably saved you from an amputation . . . " This time it was Cressida's turn to look dumbfounded.

Arthur knew it was time to beat a tactical retreat. "Do you know, Wantage, I believe that we should go and have our lunch, I'm sure I heard Mrs Plunkett bringing it in." He took the somewhat surprised doctor by the arm, propelling him towards the door . . . "I'm sure these two young people have something they want to say to each other and we should leave them to it . . . "

Mike was the first to speak, his voice incredibly deep and tender. "Come on, Cressy, the truth at last — was it really thirty-six hours?"

"I suppose it was, I rather lost track of time."

"And you stayed with me for every one of them . . . ?"

"Oh, don't you understand, Mike, I love you so much . . . you just had to live . . . and you seemed to need me then . . . "

"I've always needed and loved you, my darling, from the first moment I saw you . . . " And at last they were in each other's arms and this time the kiss reached the completion that had been denied the first time, and to Mike it was the absolute confirmation that to the one person in the world that mattered, he was indeed a 'whole man'.

He held her close and she buried her face in his chest and could feel his heart beating and knew it was all for her. Then she lifted her eyes to meet his. "I think you'll have to tell me now about that episode in the church." So he did — but it took rather longer than it might have done because he kept interrupting the story by kissing her and then he took her hands between both of his and gently asked if she would be his wife. "But can I ask you to wait till I can walk down the aisle without crutches?"

"My darling Mike, I can wait . . . well until you're out of plaster at least!" she added mischievously.

He smiled, then looked at her very seriously, his sea-green eyes deep with emotion. "I must ask you once again, are you absolutely sure about marrying a crip . . . "

"Shhhh, my darling." Cressida put a finger to his lips. "Don't . . . to me you have never, ever, been anything but the man I love, the man I want to marry, the man I want to be the father of my children."

"You don't think they'll mind that I'll never be able to play cricket with them?"

"They might all turn out to be girls and that would be much worse!"

"Why?" He sounded anxious.

"I can't knit!"

"Come on, stupid," he said fondly. "I think it's about time that we went and told your father, who, incidentally, is one of the wisest men I know, that his youngest and most beautiful daughter has got herself engaged to be married."

★ ★ ★

April had come again, and Tom and Julia were making sedate progress towards Dunster, where a wedding was about to take place. Sedate, because Tom was driving the Jag and despite its potential speed he was unaccustomed to driving with the modifications that had been made to accommodate Mike's disability. There were two other reasons: Lucy and Andrew were strapped into the tiny rear seats and required frequent stops for refreshment.

Tom pulled into the familiar service-station. The children tucked into ice-cream while he and Julia had a coffee. He was playing idly with the car keys, when suddenly Julia asked, "Could I see those for a minute please?" Tom put them into her outstretched palm and she began to examine them closely, or rather to examine the blue enamel fob that Cressida had also noticed. "Do you know where Mike got this?"

"I've really no idea. I know it means a lot to him though — a couple of years ago he thought he'd lost it and made us turn the yard inside out! You remember, Lucy?"

"Yes, 'cos I found it. It was down behind the sofa in Daddy's flat. Uncle Mike gave me a whole pound for finding it."

"Why does it interest you so much?"

Tom was curious.

"I'm not sure really, it reminds me of something I once nearly gave Cressida . . . "

"How can you 'nearly give' someone something," Lucy wanted to know.

"It was for her eighteenth birthday, a powder-compact with her monogram in silver on blue enamel, just like this," she held it out for Tom to look at. "It got lost before I could give it to her though."

"But those are Mike's initials — M. C."

"They could be Cressy's too, a C and an M. With a monogram you can't always tell which way round they're meant to be."

"If you're so interested you'll just have to ask him about it when we get there. Which we never will if we don't get a move on. Come on you two, let's go." Julia spent the rest of the journey deep in thought.

The greetings were hardly over before Julia took her sister aside. "Can we go and talk somewhere?"

Cressida suggested her bedroom. "Well! What's so important . . . and secret?"

"I don't know that it's either but there's something I have to ask you and I thought you might prefer to give me the answer in private, that's all."

"Fire away," her sister smiled.

"It's about what happened the day before your eighteenth birthday, I'm sure you remember."

The smile died, Cressida was never likely to forget. "Do you have to bring that up now?"

"Yes, I think I do. I really need to know exactly what happened to that package I asked you to collect for me — the one you said you'd 'lost'. Was it stolen, or did you leave it on the bus, or drop it, or what?"

What did it matter now, Cressida thought, it was all so long ago; but if Julia wanted to know so badly . . . She turned away as she recounted the whole story. It was perhaps fortunate that she didn't see the changing expressions on her sister's face as her tale unfolded.

When she had finished, Julia let out a little squeal. "My God! I've got to go and see Mike!"

Cressida turned round. "Whatever's the matter, Julia?"

"Don't worry, sis. I promise you everything's going to be all right and you'll know about it very soon — but I *must* speak to Mike first. Don't go away."

Barely waiting for an answer to her knock, Julia burst into his room. "I'm sorry, Mike, I've just got to talk to you . . . I think I've just discovered something incredible . . . I haven't told Cressy yet because . . . "

"Hold on there, Julia! . . . slow down a minute! Take a seat and then tell me what all the excitement's about?"

"Has Tom given you your car keys yet?" Mike nodded and fished them out of his pocket. It was an unexpected request. Her next remark was even more surprising. "I am right in thinking that you've never told Cressida what happened when you had your accident?" He frowned inclining his head . . . "and I can assure you that Tom has never spoken to me about it. Now I'm going to tell you a story that I have only just heard and then you can say how much of it you already know.

On June 14th, six years ago, Cressida was coming home from Arbury; it was the eve of her eighteenth birthday and I had asked her to collect a package from the jewellers for me. She decided to go and have a look at the cars practising at the Brandstone circuit, it's quite close to here, you know." Julia could see that she had more than gained Mike's interest now. "She had a secret place where she could watch the track without being seen, but she hadn't even reached it when a vintage sports car came off the track and practically landed at her feet. The driver was trapped underneath and bleeding from a terrible wound in his leg." Julia's dramatic talents were now coming to the fore as Mike's jaw tensed. "Cressida used the nearest things she could find to apply a pressure-bandage, then the rescue party arrived and she slipped away before anyone saw her . . . "

Mike could contain himself no longer. "You're telling me that it was Cressida who? . . . But I don't understand . . . How do you know all this? . . . It seems impossible . . . "

"I haven't finished yet. Someone must have kept that," she pointed to the fob he was still holding, "as a souvenir for you. You must have been amazed to find your initials on it but really they are Cressida's, and I know because I had it designed specially for her, although it was then the lid of a silver powder-compact . . . wasn't it?"

There was no reply. Mike was stunned into silence, then he said slowly. "So I owe my life, not once but twice, to Cressida. How can I repay her?"

"Oh Mike, you mustn't think of it like that! A great shadow in her life will

242

be lifted. You see she always believed that the driver she tried to save had died and that somehow it was her fault . . . I must call her now, you must be the one to tell her."

Later, when everybody had heard the whole story, of course it had been quite easy to work out the sequence of events, once all the facts were known. The driver who had died had been involved in a completely unconnected accident; Mike had never been in the local hospital, he had been flown by helicopter straight to the orthopaedic unit at Boroughfield.

* * *

Cressida lay encompassed by the warmth and strength of Mike's arms, supremely happy at last in the fulfilment of their love. Dawn was breaking and she nestled closer as she listened to the birds' chorus. Mike stirred in his sleep and cupped his hand round her breast with an unconscious possession. In her mind she relived her wedding-day — a day that had had its own share of surprises.

Although the marriage was not till the afternoon, Cressida couldn't stay in bed. From her window she had seen their Uncle Charles arrive, he was to 'give her away'. But she thought he would be rather in everybody's way at this hour. Mrs Plunkett had come in to collect the breakfast-tray and announced that Cressida was wanted at the church for another rehearsal.

"But surely we did all that yesterday!"

"I know, dear, but your Uncle Charles insists ... and put on a pretty dress and some make-up ... it wouldn't do for any of your Dad's parishioners to see you looking untidy on your wedding day."

She found Mrs P. waiting to accompany her down the orchard path to the church. There they were met by Julia, their uncle and the two children. Before she could say anything Charles took hold of Julia's arm and Lucy and

Andrew fell in behind them. "You follow us, Cressida my dear, then you can see exactly how it should be done this afternoon."

As they entered the inner door, and Cressida saw Tom and Mike standing by the chancel steps, but with Tom nearest to the aisle, the penny suddenly dropped. It wasn't a rehearsal at all, but another wedding! "Oh Julia!" she exclaimed. At the sound of her name Julia looked back and gave her astonished sister a wink and a grin. The ceremony was just as moving as her own was to Mike later in the day, but she couldn't help feeling a little sad that her beautiful sister hadn't had the glamorous affair she'd always imagined. Julia didn't even want the guests at her sister's wedding to know but Cressida was having none of that.

"You've got to tell them at the reception, Julia . . . and if you don't I will! Then, at least, we can share the cake."

Her own wedding had been everything

she had ever dreamed of. She had worn a dress of pale-cream silk and her mother's veil, the bouquet of creamy stephanotis and carnations had arranged within it four red rosebuds. Round her neck she wore Mike's blue enamel fob, suspended from a new silver chain which had been Julia's special gift. It symbolized not only the age-old tradition of 'something old, something new, something borrowed and something blue' but also the very life of her husband. And yet for Cressida the greatest joy of all came as they were leaving the vestry. Mike had turned to Tom and handed him the single crutch he still used, then smiling down at his new wife he had tucked his arm into hers for their journey back down the aisle — he didn't say anything but she knew that it was his gift, his gesture of acceptance. She gave one glance back at the great east window and smiled.

Mike woke, and saw that she too was awake. "Tell me what you're thinking," he murmured, his breath warm against her cheek.

"I can't!"

"Why?" His hand moved down and caressed her hip.

"They haven't invented the words yet."

"For what?"

"For saying how much I love you!" She moved to face him.

"Then tell me without words, my darling," he said softly as their lips met.

THE END

Other titles in the
Linford Romance Library

SAVAGE PARADISE
Sheila Belshaw

For four years, Diana Hamilton had dreamed of returning to Luangwa Valley in Zambia. Now she was back — and, after a close encounter with a rhino — was receiving a lecture from a tall, khaki-clad man on the dangers of going into the bush alone!

PAST BETRAYALS
Giulia Gray

As soon as Jon realized that Julia had fallen in love with him, he broke off their relationship and returned to work in the Middle East. When Jon's best friend, Danny, proposed a marriage of friendship, Julia accepted. Then Jon returned and Julia discovered her love for him remained unchanged.